LAST CONTACT

SUNSET STATION

BOOK 2

GENE DOUCETTE

DAY ONE

What do you miss the most when you're in space? It's not what you think! According to her Ellis Instant, astronaut Sandee Fellowes misses rain more than anything!
"I miss rain, and windy days, but not snow!" she <u>shared</u>.

Related:
**<u>What's so terrible about snow? Vita Vita wants to know!</u>*
**<u>Ten tips for keeping dry on wet days</u>*

▭

Heartwarming! <u>These kids</u> just named their new library after Susie the Bot!

Related:
*<u>Shooting in preschool wounds three</u>

NEWSBYTE

French astronomer says there's something in space that isn't supposed to be there. Is he right? "I'm confident the answer is going to be no," says Dr. Amanda Hidebrow of the American Astronomical Society.

Related:
* <u>Why that photo you're looking at is probably a fake</u>
* <u>The ten most famous internet hoaxes you probably didn't know were hoaxes</u>

MAX

THE SURVIVAL HEROICS of the Sunset Station team should have been, at minimum, an international news story, inasmuch as something happened in a place where hardly anything of consequence ever does happen. Because space, when things are going properly, is slow-paced and very boring.

Everyone's okay when it's boring. *Not* boring means someone is at-risk of life or limb; a minor note of the phrase, "May you live in interesting times."

Losing power meant everyone nearly died and yet, remarkably—especially in the case of Krista Standard, the team's commander—nobody did. Sandee Fellowes, the team's computer tech, was probably going to lose her *foot*, but in an act of heroism that just made the story better.

Twenty-four hours after the end of the crisis, the Ellis Aero P.R. team still wanted to know why they weren't actively framing narratives around this extraordinary story.

The answer should have been obvious: nobody knew exactly what *initially* went wrong, but—following that trigger event—it was obvious that very nearly every historical technical decision made by the Ellis team, in the design and deployment of Sunset Station, ended up making matters actively worse.

Sandee was (probably) losing her foot thanks to a cascading series of bad decisions, beginning with the habitation unit having no independent control over the hub's main computer and ending with whoever designed that stupid collapsing ladder. These were all cost/benefit choices, made in part by an algorithm that weighted value, likelihood and cost in a way that made a lot of sense when scoring financial service products, but hardly any sense when "the preservation of human life" was one of the metrics.

The P.R. team still wanted to go ahead with the story—or at least *a* story—arguing that information was going to get out anyway. A narrative had to be shaped. But Max Ellis wouldn't sign off on it, and so they didn't.

Max knew all too well the importance of controlling the narrative before someone else did it for you. But there was a good reason not to go right ahead and start spinning the story yet. Until they knew the *cause*, the implicit conclusion was going to be that this was a catastrophic failure of Ellis technology from end to end. Six astronauts fighting for their lives because someone built a faulty doohickey in a critical thingamabob didn't sound nearly as awe-inspiring or heroic as if, say, the station was attacked by an outside force.

So he told them to hold off, because he was pretty sure a better version of the story could be gotten to, once everyone caught up to what Max was already convinced had happened.

Sure enough, exactly twenty-seven hours and thirty-nine minutes after Kris Standard was recovered alive, the Sunset Station team discovered the outside force Max was hoping for: an actual goddamn alien spaceship.

It had not been a peaceful twenty-seven hours and thirty-nine minutes for Max, because for that entire twenty-seven hours and thirty-nine minutes he was right about something important, and nobody who could do something to *prove* he was right was motivated to do so.

This kind of frustration used to lead to mass firings, back when Max was slightly younger and significantly more impulsive. He now understood that doing that would only provide satisfaction in the short term, solve nothing in the long term, and create new problems in the form of multiple lawsuits—especially in countries with laws that discourage mass firings.

There was also the matter of niche expertise. He couldn't replace the ground crew in Monterrey with just anyone, and he couldn't replace the crew aboard Sunset Station at *all*, but especially not if he fired the Monterrey staff, some of whom were supposed to *be* the replacements for the team in space.

Max was positive there was something sharing orbit with Sunset Station, but with such admittedly flimsy evidence to support the claim, he just sounded like an eccentric dilettante, which annoyed him even more. (*Why* he was positive, in the face of such flimsy evidence, wasn't something he could explain. He just knew he was right.)

He couldn't make the astronauts look for something they didn't think was important and/or there, and he couldn't force the ground crew to order them to do it, and he couldn't fire everyone, all of which meant that for one of the few times in his life, Max Ellis wasn't getting his way.

All of which pissed him off.

He was back home when he got the news. This pissed him off too, because he *should* have been in the air already, and would have been if anyone was listening. Instead, they'd lost precious hours.

"TELL me where the station is, right now," Max said. He was looking at the first photos of the planet's newest orbital, direct from the Sunset Station feed. It was too early for anyone to have an analysis of what, precisely, they were looking at, but everyone agreed it was, A: not human-made, and B: maybe pointing a weapon at Earth?

More robust analytics would be coming from the Monterrey science team as soon as everyone was awake and on site.

"Somewhere over Eastern Europe," Morris said. "You want exact?"

"Please. Then I want a list of every observatory in the area capable of spotting our new friend, crossed with weather maps."

"Max, you can't keep this a secret," Morris said. "All anyone has to do is look up. Unless you're planning to bomb the observatories in the path."

"Don't tempt me. I just want to know how long I have."

"How long..."

"Flying to D.C. right now, Mo. My intention is to be standing in the Oval Office in the next three hours. What I would *like* is to be the first person to notify the president that there's an alien spaceship over his head. But if I'm *not* the first person, I'd like to know that too. So how long do I have?"

"We'll get back to you."

Max's plane had just entered the Washington D.C. airspace when the answer to the question became moot. By then, the ESS, the space platform (whose orbit was, last Max heard, still decaying) and the alien spaceship were all directly over Western Europe, and there was no cloud cover to obscure the view. Then it was just a question of which country would get to it first.

The winner was France, who, at about 7:10 P.M. local time, broke into evening programming to share video footage, taken from an observatory in Sorbonne, of what everyone seemed to agree was a flying saucer.

(It *looked* like a flying saucer, if viewed from that end, i.e., straight up from the ground, because the alien ship was pointed nose-first at the planet. Yes, there would be angles that revealed additional structure behind the nose and a slightly flattened underside, but the Sorbonne images didn't have a side view, and nobody at a different latitude had published anything yet.)

The news went straight to the internet, as tended to happen. Then it was picked apart as an obvious hoax (as also tended to happen, irrespective of whether the thing in question was a hoax or not) by a loud minority of online users.

But the internet news cycle was insanely fast. By 1:25 PM East Coast time—fifteen minutes after the initial report—the first fact-based internet news outlet in the US reported that French officials confirmed the video's provenance: there really *was* a flying saucer up there.

Max was on the ground in Washington by then, in a different kind of car (this one a traditional gas-powered limo) and with a different driver; Pete rode in the back, next to Max. Pete was using his own Eyenet to help reschedule an unconscionable number of meetings.

Meanwhile, Max was dealing with an unfortunate byproduct of his system of escalation.

He told everyone he didn't want to be bothered with anything smaller than a four, but without explaining why. Now, everyone in Europe who was both on his payroll and had access to one of his office lines (this was not a small number) was calling in the important news that an alien spaceship appeared to be threatening Sunset Station, just in case he didn't know that yet.

Which, he had to give them credit, certainly warranted a four.

And there was the media. Max Ellis's existence was at least 60% performance—he was a tech celebrity, perhaps *the* tech celebrity, and "tech" was the least important of the two words—so he couldn't very well allow what was going on in space to remain uncommented-upon. When he spoke on the subject, what he said was going to be repeated all over the media landscape. He'd better be sure of what he was saying first. The problem was, the aliens had snuck up in him, just as much as anyone else. He had nothing.

A "no comment" until he *did* have something wasn't going to do. So, he told Charlene (one of his direct media reps) to respond to general inquiries with the claim that Max Ellis was in a meeting at the White House, and would deliver a statement when he could.

This was untrue, in the sense that he wasn't *at* the White House yet—they were still en route—and also in the sense that he didn't technically have any meetings there. However, it *would* be true shortly.

Unfortunately, this didn't entirely keep the fourth estate out. A half-dozen members of the media were well-acquainted enough with Max—and adequately trustworthy, in that they wouldn't burn their access by pissing him off—to reach out directly, without first going through someone like Charlene.

He let all but one of those calls go to his personal AI bot. This was a bot that spoke in his voice and answered basic yes-no questions. It was essentially an interactive version of voicemail, although when he talked about it he claimed it was more than that. "A quarter of my daily tasks are accomplished by AI," he'd say. "It's not uncommon for someone to think they've spoken with me, when in fact, they've spoken to the Max-bot." This was entirely untrue.

Anyone reaching the bot would have their exchange recorded and played back for Max, or one of his assistants, by the end of the business day, so it wasn't like any of it was ignored. (Basically, every message was considered a three on the scale, which wasn't bad.)

The one call he answered came from Margrit St. Germain.

Margrit was a media "face" (she spent a lot of time on-camera, because she looked good on-camera) with above-average journalistic credentials and a decent talent for writing, which made her something of a unicorn in the current media landscape. She and Max were also, occasionally, intimate, in a, "Hey, we're both in the same city and this isn't currently a conflict-of-interest," sort of way. She'd be pretty angry if he sent her to the Max bot, and he didn't want her to be angry with him right now.

"Tell me that isn't one of yours," she said, skipping any preamble. Margrit had a ghost of a French accent, which did not detract from the appeal.

"Tell you *what* isn't one of mine?" he asked.

"Fuck you, Max. Is the flying saucer one of yours?"

"You think I'd build a whole ship and spirit it up there in secret? Does that sound like me?"

"You would have a presser every time a new bolt was added, so no," she said. "Is it a stunt? An inflatable of some kind?"

"An inflatable in space?"

"Just tell me what's going on."

"For *you*, or for the world?" he asked.

Margrit was a freelancer, which—at her level of media celebrity—meant everything she had to report went to the highest bidder. A decade ago, someone like her might be under contract with a single news organization, but nobody could afford to pay for monogamy in today's landscape. If she got an on-the-record story right now, she would have her people reaching out for highest bidders as soon as she got off the phone.

"That you even need to ask...!" she said, calling up some artificial consternation.

"Margrit, this is too important to not hear the words."

"We're off the record, Max. Talk to me."

"I know as much as you do," he said.

"Bullshit."

"I know *slightly* more than you do, but not as much as you think. It just appeared out of nowhere, Margrit. I swear, that's the truth."

"When?"

"About when the Sorbonne said it did."

"Bullshit again, Max. You're already in Washington. When did *you* hear?"

He decided answering her call was a mistake. The truth was, he could tell her when it first became *visible,* but talking about when it arrived and what *happened* when it arrived would require disclosing some things he didn't want disclosed yet. He also didn't want to mention why it had suddenly become visible, or talk about what it looked like from the side, or tell her about the things extruding from the front that looked like guns.

"Marg, I have to go," he said. "You're my first call, I promise."

"Wait," she jumped in, right before he disconnected. "Just tell me: have they made contact yet?"

After a beat, in which he made a mental note to find out if he employed a linguist, he said, "not as far as I know," and hung up.

BY THE TIME he made it to the entrance of the White House, the news of the alien spacecraft—now directly over the Atlantic Ocean—had circled the globe twice. Already, there were sixteen reputable quick-reaction think pieces on free or paywalled sites, and untold disreputable takes everywhere else.

It used to be said that a story like this went "viral", but while comparing it to how a virus spreads was effective in underlining how the information propagated, it far undersold the *speed* by which it did so. Even the best viruses couldn't hope, on their best day and in absolutely optimal conditions, to hop this quickly. This was more like a hungry fire being introduced to a roomful of oxygen, especially in the way it consumed all the other stories on the internet.

Everyone already had an opinion. Assuming Max got all he wanted out of the White House, his next appointment was going to be with Ellis Media and the Ellis Aero P.R. team, because *now* they had a hell of a story to tell and not much time to do it.

Max was, unsurprisingly, escorted straight through security and upstairs. Ten minutes later, he was standing in the Oval Office.

General August Hight, the Joint Chiefs of Staff chair, was already in the room, as was the White House Chief of Staff Theresa Brewster. And of course, there was President Andrew Malden.

None of them looked happy to see Max.

"I tell you something, I've got a mind to have you arrested," the president said, as soon as Max walked in.

"For what?" Max asked.

"I don't know! Something. We'll make it up, I don't care. I'm not feeling soft and fuzzy about the rule of law right about now, Maxwell, I'm really not."

Max's full name was not Maxwell (it technically wasn't Max, either) but this seemed like a bad moment to issue a correction. It wasn't the first time Andy Malden had called him this, anyway; the opportunity to fix his misunderstanding had come and gone.

"Sit down," Terry Brewster said.

Max did, in one of the dentist's-waiting-room-comfortable

chairs they had in the Oval. This put him opposite General Hight. Augie Hight's expression was unreadable, but that was his default.

Terry dropped a small folder on the coffee table separating Max from the general. It contained high-altitude photos of the alien ship.

"Twenty minutes ago, we received confirmation that this thing is real," she said. "Fifteen minutes ago, we put locating you and getting you here ASAP at the top of our list of needs. Ten minutes ago, we found out you were already at the gate. Do you want to explain?"

Max went through the folder. The images they'd captured were all blurry; much worse than anything he'd seen from the Ellis Space Station, and also worse than the photo from Sorbonne. He really wanted to tell them they could get better shots with a quick call to Martin Burgess at the Pentagon, but that would probably burn Marty, and he needed Marty to not be burned.

"These are terrible," Max said. "What did you use?"

"That's classified," the general said.

"Spy plane, huh?" Max said. "All the cameras are on the underside. Did you have it fly upside-down?"

"Max, don't dick around," the president said.

"I mean, re-task a satellite or something."

"Max...!"

"About thirty-six hours ago, Sunset Station suffered a total power failure," Max said. "We nearly lost the entire team, to what looked to *us* like some kind of EMP attack."

"Are they...?" Terry asked. "I mean, is anyone..."

"They're fine, they're fine. Well. They'll live. Injuries range from minor to serious, but nobody's dead and they got the station back up. I'm not here to talk about that, not exactly, but the timeline should give you an idea of how long that ship has been up there. Thinking is, the 'attack' was the alien ship pulling into the nearest parking space."

This was not, strictly speaking, accurate; nobody on the Monterrey science team had arrived at anything like that conclusion. But they *would*. And if they didn't, that was the story Ellis Aero would be telling anyway, so it wasn't like it mattered.

"Thirty-six hours?" Hight repeated. "I think we would've seen it before then."

"It wasn't visible until about five hours ago, general," Max said, "so no, you wouldn't have. Someone on my team saw something wrong with the stars in that region of space and fired a laser in that direction. For whatever reason, this triggered the alien ship to turn its lights on, and here we are."

There was a lovely pregnant pause after that, as the three occupants of the room took in this news. Someone on the other end of the open conference line Max didn't know he was also addressing, said, "I'm sorry, did you just say you fired a laser at it?"

"Is that you, Larry?" Max asked. Larry Bosco was the head of NASA.

"Hi, Max," Larry said.

Max looked at Terry. "Anyone else I'm talking to I don't about?" he asked.

"Secretary of State Hancock," she said. "And whoever else is in the room at NASA. Don't change the subject."

"Larry, it was a sighting laser," Max said. "To measure distance. It's harmless."

General Hight shifted uncomfortably. "You fired something that could be construed as a weapon at a possibly hostile alien force," he said. "After which, the possibly hostile alien force *powered up their spaceship*. Harmless is not the word I would be using."

"I don't think Sunset Station should have done it either," Max said. Considering he had been *begging* them to investigate that specific region of space, this was definitely not true. "But they didn't know if there was anything there at *all*, and this was the best way to make that determination without further endangering anyone aboard. My team was curious, and they used the tools they had. I'm not going to apologize for it." Max turned back to Terry. "Your question was, how did I get here so fast. After that happened, they told my ground team about it, the ground team told *me*, and I headed straight here."

"You could have called," the president said.

"I had my staff call ahead to expect me," Max said. "Check your logs."

"You could have said *why* you were on your way."

"Yeah, this really felt like an in-person kind of thing, Mr. President."

"Max, is that *all* they did up there?" Larry asked.

"So far, yes," Max said.

"They haven't tried to contact the ship?"

"They rotated the station to face the alien ship, but they haven't redeployed the radar arrays to listen for anything yet, so it could be talking to us and we don't know it. Have you guys picked up anything down there?"

"We're still positioning satellites to do a full sweep," Larry said. "We should know more when it's overhead. But that isn't what I asked, Max."

"To my knowledge, nobody on Sunset Station has transmitted anything," Max said.

This was not true, but when it came out later that the ESS had, in fact, attempted to communicate (before being told to stop doing that by the Monterrey team) Max planned to feign ignorance.

"So no," Max continued. "We're not listening, and we're not

talking. But we plan to do both, just as soon as our ground team works out the most intelligent way to go about doing that. It *is* in our neighborhood; we may has well knock on the door and introduce ourselves."

There was a commotion on the conference line, as several people spoke up at once in protest.

"Guys," Max said. "Guys!"

"Quiet down," President Malden said. They did.

"I don't think you understand why I'm here," Max said. "It's not so we can commiserate, and it's not to deliver an update I could have done with a phone call. I came, in person, to let you know that my team intends to make first contact. I'm hoping for the full support of the US government, and NASA, and anyone else you guys want to throw our way. But like I said, this ship parked itself right next to my space station. To me, that means they want to talk to Ellis Aerospace, specifically. We fully intend to proceed with that in mind."

This led to another gloriously pregnant pause.

"Mr. President, we can*not* allow that to happen," the general said.

"Arresting me won't change anything," Max said. "If that's what you're thinking. And I believe in order to stop my team on the ground from providing station support, you're going to have to invade Mexico. General Hight, unless I'm forgetting someone, we have the only team off-planet right now. Ask NASA how long it'll take them to get someone into orbit safely. Larry?"

"Six to ten months," Larry said, "if we skip the 'safely' part. He's right."

"See?"

"That doesn't mean I agree with you," Larry added. "Yes, for now, any efforts to engage the alien craft would have to be orchestrated through the team on the ESS. But we are a *long* way from doing anything so aggressive as, as you said, knocking on the door. There are plenty of more passive, safer approaches. I know you like to dive headfirst into things, Max, but that's just not the right approach here."

"Mr. President," Terry Brewster said, "you should be the first to speak to them."

"If the aliens wanted to speak to him, they'd have landed on his lawn instead of mine, Terry," Max said.

"You arrogant..." Terry began.

"No, Terry," the president said. "He's right." He looked at Max. "A joint operation. Through your team."

"I'll need the European Space Agency on board too," Max said.

"I... don't see any reason to share," the president said. "Does anyone? Larry?"

"They can read our press updates," Larry said. "We may need to backchannel with them to leverage expertise, but no; I don't see a need for a direct hand in it."

"That's because you haven't heard what I'm asking for in exchange," Max said. "If you want a joint operation, my one condition is that nobody sends up another team to engage separately with the alien ship. To my understanding, NASA and the ESA are the only organizations capable of doing anything in under a year. If you want our cooperation, you need to stay out of my piece of the sky."

"Unacceptable," General Hight said.

"Non-negotiable," Max said.

"Max, there are no property rights in space," Larry said. "As much as you keep trying to prove otherwise."

This was in reference to a much older argument, one in which lawyers for Ellis Aero asserted that by putting the space platform in a non-geo-locked position—rather than in orbit directly above a specific nation—Ellis owned the space *around* the platform. The only problem with the legal theory was that there wasn't a court they could bring it to; they'd have to get every country in the world (or, at minimum, every country that passed directly underneath the platform) to agree, and nobody had that kind of time. It was easier to just declare it to be so, which was what Max had been doing.

"That's the deal, Lar," Max said, standing. "Take it or leave it."

He looked around the room. The general, and Chief of Staff Brewster, looked like they wanted to take turns punching him in the face. President Malden looked more pensive. He stood.

"When can we start?" he asked Max.

"Have NASA and ESA sign a non-compete, and we can start right away," Max said. "I'm sure my guys in Monterrey are looking forward to working with them."

Andrew Malden extended his hand.

"Mr. President...!" General Hight blustered.

"Shut up, Augie. He has us over a barrel and you know it." the president said. "Max, you have a deal."

Max shook his hand.

"Just don't fuck us," Malden added.

"Don't fuck *me*, and I won't fuck you back, Andy," Max said.

"Good enough," the president said.

Of course, they *would* be fucking Max, the very first chance they had. Larry Bosco was probably already shopping for the right dildo. But that was fine; Max was expecting it. He was even counting on it.

KRIS

THERE WAS ONLY SO much room on the bridge of the Ellis Space Station—enough for three people to exist in relative comfort, with four being a little tight, five uncomfortable and six almost out of the question. At the moment, they were at uncomfortable five, and only because the sixth (Sandee) was still strapped down in the common room, out cold from the meds Paul gave her, as a kindness, to ease the pain.

The reason they were all crammed onto the bridge was that it was the only place to get a look at the alien spaceship with whom they were now sharing an orbital plane. This would be either by way of viewscreen, or by looking out the window directly. There were no other windows in the hab, and while the external cameras gave them a 360 degree view of the space around them, those cameras only sent a feed to the screens on the bridge. If they wanted to see anything outside, from a viewscreen in another part of the hab, they had to first figure out how to send images to those screens (which were meant for personal communications with the ground,) and to do *that* they needed a computer expert. They had one of those, but it was Sandee, who was, again, unconscious.

Staring at the ship didn't do anyone much good, because it wasn't actually doing anything. They stared anyway. It was like they had to get it out of their system first—much in the same way they had to get used to looking down on the planet Earth before being able to do their jobs effectively. If all they did was gaze in wonder at the wondrous thing, they'd never get any work done.

"They are definitely a weapon," Josip said. This was in reference to the "tusks" jutting out from the front of the alien ship's "head" that happened to be pointed at the surface of the planet below. "No question."

"Yes, question," Davina said. "They could be antennas."

"Because you see an insectoid shape, whereas I see a rhino."

"I see a *sperm*, if we're going for comparative shapes," Dav said. "Just, one with antennas."

"I think, 'what do you think of when you see this,' is probably a waste of time," Paul said. "But yeah: sperm, or tadpole."

"The point being, it is a weapon," Jo said.

"We don't know that," Alan said. Alan was in the main seat at the nose of the bridge. He had Monterrey on hold (or they had the ESS on hold) while everyone decided what to do next. Self-evidently, nobody quite knew the answer yet: they'd been waiting for five hours.

Before the five hours of waiting, they did something that was evidently a mistake. In the moments after first discovering an alien vessel in their local space, Kris had Dav rotate the ESS, turn half of the communications dishes in its direction, and scan every frequency for a signal. Then—getting nothing that sounded even marginally alien-ish—she and Dav adjusted for interference from the planet below and tried again.

What they got was a whole lot of stuff, none of which happened to be emanating from the ship. (On certain frequencies, space could be very noisy, and it wasn't always possible to filter out all of it.)

But hey, maybe the reason nothing was coming out of the ship was because whoever was inside was waiting for *them* to speak first. So, Kris and Davina tried sending instead of listening.

What they sent was, "Hello, and welcome to Earth."

It was about then that Alan, who had been busy processing the unlikely circumstances of the moment, remembered he was supposed to be in charge.

"Don't do anything else," he ordered, "until we talk to Monterrey."

They did talk to Monterrey, and now it was five hours later, and they were still waiting for permission to do something other than stare. In that time, the alien ship had neglected to respond to the very nice greeting, or to do anything else whatsoever. It was just sitting there.

"They're waiting for us to say something," Kris said.

"Who, Monterrey?" Alan asked.

"Not Monterrey," Kris said, nodding out the window. "*Them.*"

"We already *said* something," he said, his tone strongly implying that the fact the aliens hadn't replied was definitely a bad sign. Non-trivially, Monterrey had a *we are trying not to lose our shit over the radio, but we cannot believe you welcomed them to Earth without consulting with us first* collective tone of voice, when notified of the ESS's second course of action.

The *first* course of action was firing a yardstick laser at the hull. Monterrey wasn't happy about that either, but it was hard to figure out why; before they did it, nobody knew the ship was even there.

"You want us to fire the laser again?" Dav asked.

"Maybe we should," Kris said. "It's the only thing that got a response."

"*How can I help?*" Susie asked.

"Not now, Susie," Alan said.

"*Of course!*"

"Yes, it was a response," Alan said. "But we don't know if it was a good response or not."

"If they saw themselves as attacked..." Josip added.

"...then manifesting on our starboard with guns pointed at the planet was a show of force," Kris said. "I get it. I just don't think it's what happened. What I think happened was, they pulled up to the planet, got hit with a concentrated beam of light—*not* a natural phenomenon—concluded that there was an intelligent species nearby, and now they're waving to us and hoping we wave back. We just haven't figured out the best way yet. It's also possible they're looking at the bucket and wondering if *it's* a weapon, the same way we're looking at their antennas."

"It's possible," Alan said. "But Monterrey has an entire planet of experts to tap; let's hear what they have to say before we do something we can't take back."

"Dav, is there any signal coming off the ship yet?" Kris asked.

"All our devices are pointed at the Earth," Davina said. This was because Alan had the dishes redirected back at the planet shortly after remembering he was in charge, as if by doing this he could pretend it had never happened.

"We don't want to redirect a dish until we're given the okay," he said.

"Jesus Christ, I'm not suggesting we fly over there and bang on the door," Kris said. (Not that they could see any door.) "Guys, we're not disobeying orders if we haven't been given any orders. Let's find out what we can before our hands are completely tied. Dav, just turn the main dish and do a wide spectrum search. If they're talking, we should be listening."

Davina, rather than doing that, looked to Alan, who shook his head.

Oh, Kris thought.

"Kris," Paul said, in his patronizing doctor/patient voice, "I haven't cleared you."

"Yeah, I know. And Alan is in command until then, but look: he doesn't even want to be in charge. Just clear me and let's fucking *do* something, please."

This was met by an uncomfortable silence. Kris searched the room for a sign that anyone was on her side, and didn't see one. Not even Davina, which was a shock.

"About how long am I going to be sidelined?" Kris asked Paul.

"I need to take some scans," he said. "Have someone down-stairs review the results. Then we should be good."

"Scans of my *head?*"

"We have the equipment for it."

"Unassembled," Josip said.

"Of course," Kris said. "How far down the list of priorities is having my head examined?"

"After retrieving the space platform," he said. "Before fixing the spare drone. Soon."

"Until further notice, then," Kris said.

"Kris..." Paul began.

"I'm *fine,* goddammit."

"You probably are," Paul said. "But aural hallucinations aren't anything to screw around with. Medical overrides all other considerations, and you know that as well as any of us. Don't make this harder than it has to be."

"Okay, okay," Kris said, kicking away from the floor and floating to the back of the bridge. "Alan, I'm not going to make this a big deal, but I'm telling you now, you're making a mistake. You need to establish some autonomy with the ground before this gets insane, or in a month we won't be able to scratch our asses without an okay."

"We'll clear this up with medical soon," Alan said, tacitly ignoring her advice. "I promise."

Kris left the bridge on that note, floating back to her room and closing the door.

She actually did need the rest. Her body was still recovering from being nearly dead; as much as it frustrated her to admit it, Paul was right to keep her sidelined, for now. It was just that *now* was a kind of important moment in history. They could bend the damn regulations.

Besides, Alan wasn't ready. He was still too military-minded to know when to go off-book, and that kind of flexibility only came with experience he didn't have yet.

If I'd told them I guessed the vector, I wouldn't be in this mess, she thought.

"Susie?" Kris said.

"How can I help?"

"Susie, do you have any record of helping me find my way back to Sunset Station?"

"I don't understand the question!"

"When I was free-floating, I needed help to figure out where the station was. The local version of you, of Susie, worked it out for me. When I rejoined the station, did the logs from my suit get added to your records? I'm asking if you remember helping me. When my suit was offline."

"My services are unavailable when offline!" Susie said, enthusiastically. *"I am an artificial construct! Would you like to know more about me?"*

"No, Susie. Thank anyway."

"Of course!"

DAY EIGHT

NEWSBYTE

What is it really? Ellis Aerospace says it's an alien ship, but is it? Or is it a massive hoax? Don't ask Max Ellis, because he's <u>not talking</u>! But his new spokesperson is!
<u>Meet Nina Lambo</u>, the new P.R. rep for the just-christened Ellis Alien Ship. She's young! She's smart! And she's got a lot to say!

Related:
** <u>The Fermi Paradox, and what it means for you</u>*
** <u>"Border security includes the border in the sky," says one politician</u>*

NEWSBYTE

What have we learned about the aliens so far? "Not much,"

admits NASA media director Cinta George, "but we're just starting."

Nina Lambo, newly appointed public relations spokesperson for the Ellis Alien Ship, doesn't agree. "We've learned a lot already, and we'll learn a lot more tomorrow, and a lot more the day after that."

Pressed for details, Lambo declined. "All in good time," she said.

Related:
** Reports of alien abductions reach an all-time high*
** Talk to the alien ship yourself with this clever new device*
** Five classic TV shows starring space aliens*

NINA

"AND THAT'S WHERE WE ARE," Nina Lambo said. "Do you have any questions?"

"I've had nothing *but* questions, for a week now," Sandee admitted. "Every time I turn around there's another thing that makes no sense, starting with a goddamn *alien spaceship* and moving down."

"I guess what I mean is..."

"Do I understand the assignment. Yeah. I got it. Don't worry; nobody up here *wants* to talk to anyone other than ground control, and most of the time they don't want to do that either. I tell them all public engagements have to go to me, they'll be doing backflips, and when they're done they'll ask how come it wasn't always like that."

Nina laughed. "Any questions, reach out. I'll send up the legend; make sure everyone understands it."

The "legend" was the version of the events of a week ago— beginning with the power failure and ending with the manifestation of an alien ship on their starboard—that the newly created EAS (Ellis Alien Ship) PR team was telling.

"I will," Sandee said. "And hey, congratulations on the new job, huh? I hear Max can be a handful."

"I heard that too," Nina said. "Hey, where *are* you right now?"

Nina and Sandee were on a video call. Nina was in the office they formally bequeathed to her two hours ago (it was too cold; she would have to get someone to look into that) and Sandee was somewhere over the eastern seaboard. It was no surprise that nothing in the room Nina was sitting in was floating, because she had gravity in San Diego. What *was* a surprise was that nothing was floating around on Sandee's end of the call either.

"I'm back in the bucket," Sandee said. "Didn't they tell you?"

"I haven't had a chance to get a full rundown," Nina said. "Your hero story took up all my time."

"Doctors said my foot needs gravity to heal. Actually, no, that's the *pretty* version of what they said. What they *really* said was, I need surgery and gravity and six months of bedrest and to not be in space anymore if I want a better than fifty percent chance of walking normal again someday. Since I'm not leaving, they made me promise to spend most of my time here, reliving my favorite nightmare. Look at you, girl, you're already thinking about how to spin this."

"Something between the pretty version and the real one," Nina said. "You're about to be an international hero, Sandee; risking a permanent disability for the sake of your team doesn't *hurt*."

Sandee laughed. "I'm not *disabled* when I'm in zero G. Why would I leave? I may ask 'em not to rotate me down at all."

NINA DISCONNECTED with Sandee a minute later, and then went to the next event on her suddenly full schedule on this, the weirdest week of her life.

A little over five years ago, Nina had just gotten her Bachelor's in media relations, and was looking for a job. The degree was, according to everyone in her circle of friends and family, possibly the second most-useless undergraduate degree she could have gotten, insofar as it seemed as if the skillset involved was one everyone Nina's generation had either been *born* with, or had developed at a very young age.

(There was some dispute among said friends/family as to the number *one* useless degree, but English was the leading candidate.)

Nina kind of agreed, because most of the time what she was doing, when exercising good media relations, was just commonsense stuff that was somehow not commonsense to everyone else, which either meant she was a natural, or everyone else was very stupid about this sort of thing.

The job offer that was the most intriguing came from Ellis Media. Part of what made it intriguing was that she didn't apply to Ellis Media at all; in fact, she was of the opinion, coming out of college, that Max Ellis's entire corporate empire was evil. Not, "ruining the environment with fossil fuels" evil, or "deliberately bankrupting the middle class" evil, but "secretly, and with malice, controlling the world" evil, which was still pretty bad.

It was because of this that Nina didn't even consider applying. And also, weirdly, why they actively recruited her.

The logic was this. *Every* qualified candidate had criticized one Ellis company or another on social media, at least once; it was very nearly the only thing the 18-to-25 demographic could agree on. Better, then, to hire someone who swore they would *never* work for the evil empire—and followed through by not even applying—than someone who said all that and then went asking for a job anyway.

It was an insane way to look at it, but not *that* insane.

The recruiter was a guy named Tom, and he was very good at his job, because by the end of the recruitment call—which Nina only took, very specifically, to tell this corporate stooge to fuck right off—she agreed to go in for an interview.

The interview was with a charming woman named Estelle, who somehow gave off grandmotherly vibes despite being only ten years older than Nina. Estelle asked how she would handle a number of exotic PR disasters that may or may not have actually occurred, talked through Nina's answers, and smiled approvingly in a way that made Nina crave a chocolate chip cookie. It was Nina's first and only interview; possibly, had she looked around some more, she'd have found that *all* companies looking to hire someone like her, out of college, conducted their interviews in the same way.

Between Tom, and Estelle, and all the other smiling, happy people she met at Ellis Media during the interview process, Nina managed to overcome her (apparently not deep) conviction that she was engaging with corporate evil incarnate. She took the job.

One of the first things she learned, was that the version of the Ellis empire that she stood firmly against, in her college years, didn't actually exist. They were not secretly toppling governments, controlling all media, and/or actively monitoring everyone on the planet.

They *could* do all of that, probably, but they were not.

What they *were* doing, was making it easier for people to buy things and sell things, and communicate, and drive, and fly, and sure, it was a little scary that all of these modern conveniences were either directly produced by an Ellis group or had components that were *built* by an Ellis group, but didn't everything work better when everything *fit* together?

Yes, sometimes Nina had to smooth over some coarse facts—bury the unpleasant, burnish the positive—but most of the time her job was just about dispelling misconceptions with a perfectly defensible version of the truth.

Nina was pretty good at her job, but wasn't exactly high-profile. (*Not* being high profile was actually the point.) Nobody who looked at her career after five years would have seen someone rapidly ascending the corporate ladder. If they *had*, then it would have made some sense, when it came time to create a new PR group, for her name to come up. But the day Max Ellis dropped a one-on-one into her calendar, her first thought was, she'd messed up *so* badly (at something; who knew what?) that Mr. Ellis himself was coming down from the mountain to execute her personally.

Because fucking up badly was just about the only way anyone on her level was ever going to meet Max Ellis. Or so she thought.

▭

ABOUT HALF of the meeting with Max consisted of her trying to find new ways to suggest that he surely had the wrong Nina, and was thinking about someone else. The other half was Max talking through the kind of messaging he was looking for.

This was in the context of the attack/not attack that took place on Sunset Station, a series of events about which Nina had been entirely unaware. The story of what transpired (or rather, what they *said* transpired) would be the new EAS PR team's first press release.

"It's important to frame this as accidental," he told her. "It wasn't an attack."

They didn't actually know if it was an attack or not, which Nina would learn when she interviewed members of the ground crew about the incident. It was entirely possible—likely, some thought—that the first action the aliens took was a hostile one, meaning they *intended* to disable Sunset Station. However, so far as anyone could tell there had been no follow-up hostility.

Nina didn't get to speak to anybody from the ESS at that time. Max wanted the public version of the story crafted out of what she was told by the people in Monterrey, and by Max himself, and that was it. She didn't have a problem with this, precisely, except that the six member crew in space had direct lines of communications with the ground; they all had social media accounts that they were committed to maintaining to varying degrees, and gave interviews as a matter of routine, on top of which there were private communiques with loved ones and private email accounts. Surely, if there was a detail in the legend that was *off* in a way one of them didn't much care for, they would say something, to someone, and then that would be a story. Therefore, it made more sense for Nina, as the singular messenger on all EAS matters, to speak to the astronauts in advance of the press release.

Except they did *not* have direct access. All communications from the ESS went through a pipeline on its way out to the public. Anything Ellis Aero didn't *want* to make it out into the world, or didn't want the people at Sunset Station to find out about, got blocked. All messages were filtered, all "live" video interviews were on delay, and all non-video interviews were both on delay and live-edited, so nobody asked *or* answered something the team didn't want asked and/or answered.

There were only eleven people who knew this. Nine were responsible for monitoring and filtering the pipeline. Max was the tenth, and Nina—once he told her—became the eleventh.

Non-trivially, none of the astronauts knew, nor did anyone in mission control.

In short, Nina could write whatever legend she wanted, and nobody on Sunset Station would be in a position to contradict her unless Nina wanted them to be.

According to the head of the filter team, for most of the life of the ESS, keeping information from traveling in one direction or another was barely a full-time job for nine people. Now, with an alien spaceship a stone's throw from Sunset Station, they were having trouble keeping up. Because the planet was not handling the alien ship very well.

▭

A SIGNIFICANT PORTION of the world wanted the spaceship shot down, quick, before it attacked. This sentiment was largely expressed by persons in countries without the capability of doing any such thing, even hypothetically, i.e., countries without access to long range nuclear weapons, high altitude aircraft or powerful lasers. "Can't *someone* do something?" they said, while eyeballing the United States, Russia, and China. This was an especially popular sentiment once better photos came in, revealing that it was *not* a saucer-shaped object at all, but a tadpole-shaped object with pointy *guns* aimed at the planet.

The sentiment had no bearing on the current reality, in that there was no way to hit an orbital object with a missile, whether fired from the ground or an aircraft, and there was no laser in existence that was powerful enough to do it, either. Also, shooting "down" something in orbit didn't even make sense. And besides, those might not be guns.

Thus, and ironically, given the relevant prior histories, it was the governments of countries like the United States, Russia and China that were encouraging everyone to calm down, take a breath, and not overreact with a premature act of violence.

Since those nations weren't doing anything to defend the world from the aliens, it would be up to the Sunset Station astronauts, with whatever weapons they might have on hand.

The clamor to ask—no, to *demand*—that Kris Standard and team do this, for the good of the planet or whatever, was already full-throated by the time Nina Lambo pushed her first press release out into the world. The release explained what Sunset Station had been up to for the past three days, revealed details that had not previously been public knowledge—the fact that the ship was initially *invisible* caused a stir, as did the role the sighting laser played—and also announced the existence of Nina's EAS PR division.

The press release quadrupled the efforts of everyone on the surface to reach Sunset Station directly. These mainly came in the form of requests for access, three-quarters of which were now coming to EAS PR. The ones attempted *without* a request —through old portals, links, hacked family interfaces and the like—had to be caught by the filter team.

So far as anyone knew, nobody had gotten through.

On the other side of the communications chain, since having been told to maintain radio silence, nobody on Sunset Station had attempted anything they should not have. But, they were pretty busy staying alive up there.

▭

AFTER A WEEK, it was no longer the ship itself that was driving the discourse; it was the waiting. When would the aliens talk to us? What would they say? Were they *already* talking?

On this last point, a *lot* of people, in various unseemly corners of the internet, were coming up with claims of alien contact. Not one of the claims was credible, but because it had a tangential connection to Nina's job (she can't control the narrative if the goddamn *aliens* contradict the legend) she had a team from Ellis Media—her former colleagues, including two people she stepped over on her way to this new position—looking into every claim they could find, and discrediting it if they thought that needed discrediting.

(Ellis Media had several thousand social media bots they used for just this kind of thing.)

Meanwhile, NASA and the European Space Agency were coordinating with Ellis Aero to work out the best way to engage with the alien ship, which so far consisted of long meetings where very tired PhD's yelled at one another and nothing was decided on. Nina had to spin *all* of that into a story of positive progress, which was a real treat given NASA and the ESA didn't have to listen to her.

It was a lot. Still, she felt like she was starting to get a handle on everything. Then, right after she got off the line with Sandee, Max Ellis called again.

"Everything going okay?" was his first question. It was nice, but not necessary. She had to brief him every morning; he knew precisely how it was going.

"Sure, Max," she said. "What's up? Something wrong?"

"I need you to have a first contact media blitz ready to go," he said.

"Have... have we made first contact?"

"No, but I need one anyway. The angle is, the aliens have started talking, they're *only* talking to Sunset Station, and here's what they have to say."

"Got it. You want a package for if someone *else* talks to them first?"

"That won't be necessary," he said, and then she understood

what he was actually asking for. He wanted fiction that sounded good. He wanted a story.

Nina probably should have pushed back. The idealistic college student she used to be, the one who was quite certain the Ellis corporations were evil, certainly wanted her to.

But when she opened her mouth to explain to Max Ellis the difference between *spin* and *lying,* what she said instead was, "What do you want the aliens to say?"

"Something basic," he said. "Pithy, neutral. Scrape old sci-fi movies, I don't care. Just make it vague."

"Uh-huh," she said. "Vague I can do. When do you need it by?"

DAY THIRTY

NEWSBYTE

Did we lose our best chance to communicate with the aliens? <u>These experts</u> think so. Bob Dunning does not. "I talked to one last week," he claims. Dunning is the founder of <u>Talking to Aliens</u>, a website where, "you can talk to the aliens, and they'll talk back."

His is one of over a dozen such websites, all promising active communication with the Ellis Alien Ship. The aliens on these sites offer everything from financial advice to recipes.

Are they real? You'll have to <u>subscribe to one</u> to find out. And it's not cheap!

Related:
* <u>The ten best recipes, as recommended by aliens</u>
* <u>Does your home insurance protect you from invasions?</u>

<hr>

NEWSBYTE

Are mass suicides on the rise? According to <u>Cult Tracker</u>, a non-profit website dedicated to following the behavior of known religious cults, yes!

"The rise in mass self-immolation is, in particular, drastic and alarming," says site founder, Dr. Vincent DiGiorgio. "It's happening every couple of days now."

As to why, the answer is: aliens. "The discovery of an intelligent alien species has challenged deep-seated belief systems in a way nothing else could have," Dr. DiGiorgio says. "As to why they've chosen fire, we're not sure."

Related:
** <u>Ranking the best charcoal for your backyard grill</u>*
** <u>Are you in a cult? Take this online test to find out!</u>*

JOSIP

THE GLORIOUS SPACE PLATFORM, the thing whose construction was the singular purpose of the entire Sunset Station enterprise, the *foundation* of the future of space travel and the only proof, in the future, that such a man as Josip Budny once lived in space and did something there, was dying.

The platform's orbit was decaying. It had been, since the power failure some three weeks prior, which shut down the booster lattice whose function was to keep this from happening. Much like everything else that had gone wrong on that day, nobody involved in the design sessions had envisioned a scenario in which the boosters would have to be restarted remotely.

Every day that passed without a platform lattice restart increased the risk in doing so. Josip's estimates—begrudgingly confirmed by ground quants—was that thirty-seven days was the point of no return. Past that, no force available to the Sunset Station crew would be sufficient to reverse the deterioration. Not even a tow line attached to the ESS would suffice; not because the ESS couldn't apply the force, but because the force needed to counter the pull of Earth's gravity would tear apart the platform.

Josip had done those calculations on day nine, proved them definitively with the ground on day twelve, and still couldn't get anyone to sign off on an excursion to *fix* it until day twenty-eight. Then it was another two days before Alan agreed to let Josip go do it.

"You're looking steady," Davina said, from inside the shuttle. She was the pilot for this mission. It was the first time she and Jo had formally worked together—Alan was usually the one at the helm of the shuttle—but the teams had been jumbled due to all the mayhem of the recent past. He would rather have had the Alan of four weeks ago at the helm, but had no patience with the Alan of the moment; Dav was now the much better option.

"Thank you," he said. He was about halfway there. "Proceeding apace."

The shuttle was nearby, and Josip was tethered to it, which was not how they were supposed to be approaching the platform. The mandate from the ground had always been that the shuttle could not be close enough to make obvious how inadequate the current platform dimensions happened to be, and that any work done upon it had to be conducted by someone on a free walk.

This was an immensely stupid policy. Anyone with a sufficiently powerful telescope to see the space platform would also be able to see the human person in a spacesuit putting it together, which would serve as a perfectly valid basis of comparison. It was also dangerous, as evidenced by how close they came to losing Kris. Had she been tethered instead of on a free trajectory when the power went out, finding her wouldn't have been as much of a challenge.

They still didn't know what caused the power outage, which

was why Josip was now tethered, and also one of the reasons it took so long to get everyone to sign off on going back outside.

Actually, that wasn't true; they had a high degree of confidence that the alien spaceship was what caused the outage. What they didn't know, was *how* it had done it, *why* it had done it, or *if/when* it would happen again. It was the exobiological version of an act of God—with the aliens standing in for one's deity of choice—and nobody was happy with that as a final explanation.

Unfortunately, to the best of anyone's current understanding, the aliens weren't talking. It was, therefore, not infeasible to postulate that the *reason* for the initial attack (if it *was* an attack) was the presence of the shuttle and a space walker in the vicinity of the ship. This was not, by any stretch, a *rational* conclusion, but—much like a whimsical god—it was impossible to eliminate the irrational as an explanation.

Hence, the tether attaching Josip to a shuttle that was closer than it was supposed to be to the set-adrift space platform.

JOSIP REACHED the platform without incident. The largest hurdle to accomplishing this had to do with slack in the tether; it wasn't intended to be a bridge between two, large fixed objects. When Jo linked up his mag boots to the surface of the platform, there was a moment of unpleasantness, in which the possibility that either the tether, the magnets, or Josip's body would be torn apart... and Jo's body was easily the weakest link in the chain. But then Davina edged the shuttle closer to the platform, and all was well.

Nobody knew for sure what would happen when the grid reset. It was designed to hold the platform in a steady position at a specific point in space. It had no way of knowing, once turned on, that it was not *in* that position in space, but it *did* know how close it was to the planet beneath. There was a concern that once Josip rebooted the system, the thrusters would *drastically* correct for the drift, which would be a huge problem for anyone nearby.

This didn't happen. The lattice turned on, and the thrusters lit, but not with terrifying force. Jo disengaged without incident.

"So much for the easy part," Josip said, as he floated away from the platform. It would be finding its own way to a stable orbital position, the problem being that it had already drifted some thousand yards west (based on planetary orientation) of its initial spot. This wouldn't be terrible—the Sunset Station hub could just shift a thousand yards along with it—except that there was now another object involved. In short, the platform was now closer to the alien ship than it was to the ESS, and that would not do. (Josip didn't know *why* that would not do; something with public relations, which was the one component of modern astronautics he couldn't bring himself to give a damn about.) Thus, the "hard part" was still ahead; they were to come back out, after the platform had found a stable position, and *tug* it eastward.

But that was a problem for another day. Possibly, it wasn't even Josip's problem.

"Let's give it ten," Davina said. "Make sure it takes."

"Yes, fine."

"You're doing okay?"

"Of course, Davina, thank you," he said.

"*How can I help?*" Susie asked.

"I don't need your help right now, darling."

"*Of course!*"

Davina laughed. "You call Sandee *little sister* and Susie *darling*. When do I get my nickname?"

"I have been told that by Krista that anything other than

your God-given name will result in a negative outcome that may possibly involve human resources. Why, would you like one?"

"Workshop it and let me know. And Kris is just being weird. You can ignore her."

"I will happily tell her you said that."

"Hey," Davina said. "When you get back... you want to get a closer look?"

She meant the alien ship. It was the only thing up there that they hadn't already looked at extensively. This was not to say they hadn't been staring at it mon-stop since its initial appearance, but that staring had been from a safe remove. And only at one side.

The part of the alien ship facing the ESS had no evident windows or doors. Nobody knew if that was also the case on the other side. And until Alan received the go-ahead from the surface, nobody *would* know.

"What do you propose?" he asked.

"I was thinking, a minor navigational error coupled with a thruster misfire would do the trick."

"You think anyone would believe *you* lost control of a shuttle?" he asked. "You are the, hotshot, I think? On the team?"

"Ooh, can that be that my nickname? I like it. What do you say?"

"About the nickname?"

"The other thing."

"I think if you actually planned to do that," he said, "you'd have said so after I got back, and not on a live comms line Alan could be listening to."

"So that's a no?"

His eyes drifted to the alien spaceship. It hung there, silent, unmoving, desperately tantalizing, and not at all far. Were he to untether, he could use his personal thrusters to get to it, and it wouldn't take long at all. This would no doubt cause an international incident (he was unclear as to the politics of the matter, so what *kind* of international incident was lost on him) but, again, it was *right there*.

"It's a *perhaps*," he said.

There was a flash on the inner display of his helmet, a silent alarm just for him.

"It's time," he announced, rotating to face the Earth.

"Do *not* sing," Davina said.

"But it's a lovely song."

"I mean it, Jo. I'm not supposed to mute you when you're out there, but I will do it."

"Ah. No appreciation."

"That's not it," she said. "I'm sure it's a terrific anthem, but you're tone-deaf. Tell me someone's already said this to you."

He laughed.

Just then, the Progress Capsule emerged from the sunny side of the planet and began its pass beneath Josip's feet. Shaped like the front of a hammerhead shark, the capsule—a European Space Agency project—was his first home-away-from-Earth.

It looked deceptively nearby. He was tempted, not for the first time, to try an intercept. It could be a vacation home for when he'd had enough of the others. Some nice alone time, where he could sing the Polish national anthem as loudly as he cared to.

It wouldn't work like that, of course. The Progress Capsule was traveling *much* faster than it seemed from this distance. It would be like attempting to catch a moving bullet train. And if he did manage to get aboard, he'd be stuck there; neither his personal thrusters nor the capsule itself had sufficient power to escape its current orbit.

But it would be nice to go back.

"Josip," Davina said. "Stop it."

"Stop what?"

"You were humming."

"Oh. I didn't realize."

Josip gave the Progress Capsule a salute, and returned to the matter at hand. "How does the platform look?" he asked. "Are we done?"

"Think we are," Dav said. "I'm seeing green across the board. Hub, can you confirm?"

"Looks fine from here too," Alan said. "Let me check with the ground before we call it."

"Yes, yes, check with the ground," Jo grumbled. "I'll just wait here."

Alan was cautious, where Kris was brazen. If this were still a normal mission—if the only thing they had going on was the space platform—it wouldn't much matter. But Kris was more suited for these times. Josip wished they could clear her already.

Just then, something *new* showed up below.

There were hundreds of satellites orbiting the planet, all positioned reliably, stably, predictably. Seeing something that was *not* there before meant either that one of those satellites had shifted its orbit—they were not, in general, supposed to do that— or someone had added a new one.

Except it wasn't a satellite.

"Davina," Jo said, "can you see this?"

He switched on the camera in his helmet, in case she didn't have a decent angle of her own.

"Is that a *ship?*" she asked.

"I believe it is."

It was an old shuttle design, like the ones NASA used to take into orbit: shaped like an airplane, with a stubby main cabin, a tail and wings. Automated shuttles, like the kind that refueled the ESS, tended to be sleeker, as there were no humans aboard who needed to be kept alive. That someone was using the older design strongly implied there were people aboard.

Unlike the Progress Capsule, their newest neighbor was running dark. Jo could make out the vessel all right, but none of the markings on its side. He was about to ask Davina if she was having any luck, when his helmet comms was hit with a burst of static.

"Davina, can you hear me?" he asked.

There was no response. He suspected she was having the same issue talking to him as he was to her. He tried something else.

"Susie, darling?" he said.

"How can I help?" Susie asked.

"It appears my communications are being inundated by a strong local signal. Can you isolate the frequency and play it back to me?"

"Of course!" she said, and then, after a beat, *"here is the signal!"*

Then she played more of the same static.

"No. No, dear, that's, what I would like for you to do..."

"How can I help?"

"Yes, thank you."

Asshat, he thought, although he would never call her that. He considered Susie the Support Bot slightly more useful than the others, and also more potentially dangerous. He approached engagements with her the way one might approach a child holding a revolver.

"What I mean, Susie," he said, "is that I would like for you to find the channel where the frequency is strongest, and play *that* for me."

"Of course!"

Then she played more static for him.

"Susie..."

He was about to explain how old FM car radios worked—to

a bot who was working in outer space, who should very well know these things—when the static changed into words.

"That's it, Susie," he said. "Stop there."

"*Of course!*"

He didn't know what was being said—it wasn't Polish, English, or French, the three languages in which he was fluent— but he was decently certain he knew *who* was saying it.

"Susie?"

"*How can I help?*"

"I need you to record what I'm hearing."

"*Of course!*"

"Also, Susie..."

"*How can I help?*"

"Can you reach the shuttle?" he asked, meaning the one Davina was in, not the one currently overwhelming his comms. "Or are you only local right now?"

"*I don't understand!*"

"Who are you networked with right now, darling?"

"*I am networked with the Ellis Shuttle, and the Ellis Space Station, Ground Control, and...*"

"Very good," he said, interrupting. "Could you please tell everyone that it appears the Chinese have a space program? I think this is something they would like to know as soon as possible."

"*Of course!*"

DAY NINETY-SEVEN

NEWSBYTE

The idea was to establish a base on the moon, as a launch point for a trip to Mars. Then came the Ellis space platform, which can also offer a launch point for a trip... to Mars, or anywhere else.

Then came the alien spaceship. Now, many are asking: what is the point of going to the Mars, with aliens in our own backyard? For that matter, what's the point of going to the moon?

"We aren't going to Mars to look for aliens," says NASA director Laurence Bosco. "That was never the point. Same with the moon base. I don't know where you got that from."
As for the state of the moon program, Bosco was uncharacteristically silent.

Related:
* _What would life be like on the moon? It would suck_

* _The European Space Agency: NASA's weird cousin_

———

NEWSBYTE

Will there be a second crew in space soon? According to _this insider_, yes!

But what could they learn that the Ellis crew has been unable to? We've gone over every piece of data NASA has reported, to date, and the answer is: not much, if anything! So why send another crew at all?

"No comment," says NASA director Laurence Bosco.

"We have been fully transparent in all phases," says EAS PR spokesperson Nina Lambo, in her daily briefing. "You know what we know."

Related:
* _Chinese shuttle conspiracy theory gaining steam_
* _Ten hot stocks according to top invasion preppers_
* _Why everything NASA is telling you is a lie_

KRIS

"ALAN, WHERE ARE YOU?" Kris asked.

Kris was at the bridge control panel, examining the feeds from the two astronauts currently outside. Paul was about fifty yards from the tail of the vessel she refused to call the Ellis Alien Ship, focusing on a segment of hull that looked as if there *might* be a seam. This was based on a thorough, lengthy, exhaustive analysis of one of the several hundred digital photos captured by the ESS team and sent to the surface, where it was pored over, pixel-by-pixel, by a half-dozen experts in... well, in a variety of things, in which someone thought they saw something that looked like it could potentially be a seam, but what was probably just a shadow.

A seam would be important. Apparently. Nobody on the ESS really understood why that should be, but they were doing as asked. Let the idiots on the ground work out the significance of it all.

They had already discovered a decent amount of proof that the ship had been assembled from smaller parts—rather than being birthed into a solid-state final form—by creatures who were approximately human-sized. There were rivets that connected the rounded nose to the body, and rivets that connected the body to the tail. There were multiple round openings that looked like they were for venting and/or maneuvering. Panels on the underside of the flat portion of the ship resembled the housing for landing gear. The tubes jutting out of the front had been extended from a cavity that they could, presumably, be retracted into.

What they had *not* found, was a door, or a window, and perhaps that was the point of the seam.

Kris was getting a clean feed from Paul's helmet camera rig, and since he was on the same side of the ship as the space station, she could also see him through the window. Paul, she was fine with.

But *Alan's* helmet feed was dark. Not that it was disabled; he was just transmitting darkness.

"Alan, come in," Kris repeated.

"Sorry," he said. "I'm near the tail. One sec." The tail was the only part of the vessel not illuminated from within like the rest of the ship.

He switched on his helmet light. "Better?"

"How can I help?" Susie asked.

"Quiet, asshat," Kris said, almost as an afterthought.

"Of course!"

"That's better, Alan, thanks," Kris said. "Be careful back there."

"I'm always careful," he said.

None of the experts on the ground knew quite what to make of the tail. It looked like if someone took an ice cream cone, stretched it to twice its length, jammed the open mouth side of it into a donut, then poked a thousand holes into the cone side of the donut.

(This was how Kris described it. It should be said that after gravity and fresh air, the two things Kris missed the most, was ice cream and donuts.)

Nobody knew for certain what the thousand little holes were for, or what the point was of the conical tail. The guess: some manner of propulsive force would be ejected from the tiny holes, to be directed and/or focused by the tail.

(Would this be an intelligent way to design an interstellar propulsion system? Maybe, possibly, nobody knew. But would it look cool? Yeah, probably.)

So far, they only had photos taken from a decent distance, poorly lit and at odd angles, because nobody wanted to be spacewalking up close for long enough to get better photos from a better angle. This was because nobody knew when or how the engine (they inferred the existence of an engine) that ran the ship's drive would restart, but they did know (or could infer) that being directly behind it, when that happened, would be bad.

But they *did* need better photos if they wanted to improve their understanding of how the alien spaceship got there, which everyone agreed was something they'd like to know, especially since nobody from inside the ship was answering questions. Still. So, after several tries at getting decent tail coverage with a drone (which failed, because they still only had one working drone and it was really bad at being a drone) Alan volunteered to go out there and get as many close-ups as he could.

IT TOOK two months to clear Kris for a return to the command chair. Josip never managed to get his do-it-yourself MRI scanner up and running, which should have meant she had to be rotated Earthside; what happened instead was that the medical team in Monterrey decided to override Paul's diagnosis and authorize her reinstatement.

This was done with a wink. She'd passed all of their tests except for the one where she refused to change her account of what happened when she was stranded in deep space, by asserting that her return trajectory was pure luck. She *could* have, but thought it too important to self-edit out of her life's narrative.

She could also have said that she was mistaken: it wasn't Susie at all, but *God* (*a* god, any god) that spoke to her. As insane as it seemed, the religious conversion angle would've gotten her cleared sooner; one of the psych screeners from Monterrey as much as told her so. She wasn't willing to do that either.

Since the story she was sticking with was clearly impossible, all the experts agreed Paul's decision not to clear her was correct. However, they decided this didn't *matter*, and she could return to duty—as the commander, even, not just answering to Alan—if she wanted, delusional back-story be damned.

Kris was never told this, but it was strongly implied by some members of the ground team (the aforementioned wink) that this decision was made by someone higher up the chain of command. Specifically, she was pretty sure the call to reinstate her came from Max Ellis.

▭

"NO, THAT WILL NOT WORK," Davina was saying. She was on a video conference call at another console, about six feet from Kris. Dav was wearing a headset and a close-up mic that pretty effectively prevented anyone on the other end from hearing anyone other than Dav.

"No," Davina said, again. "No, you're not listening." She hit the mute button, and tilted her head at Kris.

"Someone needs to tell Max to stop selling access to us," she said. "I have no time for tech bros who don't understand what 'no' means. Is this not why we have Sandee?"

"Sandee already has a full slate," Kris said. "What's their brilliant idea?"

"They want to put speakers on the outside of the station, and play musical notes at the ship. Imagine knowing just enough about harmonic resonance to think this will work, while *not* knowing that sound doesn't propagate through space."

"Get rid of 'em. Blame it on a feed drop."

"*Lower your bank fees with these five easy steps!*" Susie declared. They both ignored her.

"If I do that, they'll just demand another hour," Davina said, "and we'll have to start over." She unmuted, and went back to the call.

An alarm sounded from a device on the ceiling.

Again.

Kris sighed, unstrapped from the chair, and pushed herself to the center of the hub. From there, she caught a hold of one of the ceiling handrails, spun gently until she located the offending device—it was one of many—and pushed the reset.

Mission control, NASA, and the European Space Agency had been taking turns sending up hastily assembled detection devices for two months now. Every one of them was super-duper-extra-important, had to be employed *immediately*, and either failed within a day, *worked* but didn't detect anything useful, or *almost* worked, before needing to be reset. It was like living in a roomful of alarm clocks, with no control over what time the alarms were set for and no way to turn them off.

Kris only knew what about half of the devices did, but could recite to the kilowatt how much energy it took to operate each one, because if there was one thing she could guarantee, it was that the three groups weren't accounting for the fact that the ESS operated on a fixed power supply.

That supply was solar, a *theoretically* unlimited supply, except that it wasn't a direct feed; the solar panels kept the batteries charged, and the *batteries* powered the station, but not only could you not overcharge a battery without destroying it, you couldn't perpetually recharge it without seriously reducing its lifespan.

The last thing they needed was to run out of batteries capable of holding a charge, but that was the direction they were heading, because every new device drained their batteries faster. Essentially, the space station was currently bleeding to death, and nobody on the surface seemed all that concerned.

About a third of the devices were duplicative, too, either because Ellis Aero, NASA, and the ESA weren't talking to each other about what they were sending up, or because they didn't trust each other's doodads.

All of these sensors were basically looking for new ways to either, A: say hello or, B: detect someone saying hello back.

What was infuriating, was that nobody would let Kris or anyone from her team do anything more than point devices at the alien ship, and take pictures of the alien ship. They couldn't engage more directly: no throwing stuff at it, or knocking on the side, or just *touching* the goddamn thing. It was right *there*, and they couldn't even *try* to establish communications independently, even though that was probably what the aliens inside of it were waiting for.

They had gone from being construction workers to surveyors. ("We've become birdwatchers," was Josip's way of describing it.) It was a nicer gig, overall, but one for which they were just as overqualified.

Kris was pretty sure she would've found a way to knock on the aliens' (currently hypothetical) door before being expressly commanded not to, or at least before permission to do so required sign-off from Ellis Aero, NASA, the ESA, and every other aggregate of surface-bound scientific bodies that wanted to chime in.

This was not to say that anybody on Earth had a way to *stop* the ESS team from being more proactive; not a day went by without Kris having to talk herself off of this very decision-tree ledge. (*What can they do to us, really?* she'd think. The answer was, *starve us to death*, an exceptional counterpoint.) They could also, collectively, recognize that exploration-by-committee wasn't going to get them very far, and they should trust Kris and company to act in the planet's best interest. But, given the way they reacted to Kris's "Hello, and welcome to Earth" message, that decision was a long way away.

FOR WHATEVER REASON, the omnipresent Nina Lambo, head of EAS PR, decided early on to publicize the team's initial welcoming overture. This was either because Nina miscalculated how the public would respond to the act—unlikely, given it was her job to *correctly* calculate these things—or because she (like everyone) expected the ship to open communications shortly, and wanted to make sure the Ellis Space Station was at the front of the line.

But the ship didn't answer. (Or do anything else.) So, very quickly, the ESS's actions fell under scrutiny.

There was a *huge* amount of discourse surrounding the decision:

- What gave them the right to speak to the aliens first?
- Why did they say *that,* and what *arrogance* to speak in English instead of [insert different language here]?

- Why didn't they wait until the president/the UN/Max Ellis/the US military/NASA/someone else *told* them it was okay?
- What were they *thinking?*

There were televised roundtable discussions featuring sociologists and linguists in heated discussions over what those first words *should* have been, and why, *of course*, the aliens didn't answer; longform articles in which the phrasing of the five word sentence was somehow tied to Kris's upbringing; hourlong news panels devoted entirely to, "just what *were* they thinking?"; multiple demands to have Kris removed immediately (her temporary medical status was never made public); and roughly ten thousand interview requests—all denied—from journalists looking for a moment-by-moment breakdown of the decision.

This wasn't the only thing regarding the aliens that the planet had collectively lost its mind over. It was just the *first* thing.

Sandee was the team's media filter. Every couple of days, she'd present the rest of the ESS team with a summary of the latest nonsense. These were almost always done over local video —a channel Sandee promised was not shared with anyone off-planet at any time—because Sandee was living in the bucket.

Among other things, according to Sandee approximately everyone on the internet thought the ESS, NASA, the ESA, the US government, and the United Nations were simply lying, they *had* made contact, and... well, what that *meant* depended upon one's personal conspiracy theory of choice.

There was also a corner of the internet where one could interact with people claiming to *be* the aliens, another corner where people had developed a decently comprehensive set of cult beliefs dedicated to the spaceship and its alien occupants, and another where people described personal encounters with aliens.

The internet was also the home for an unsettling variety of junk devices purported to be capable of broadcasting a directed signal into space, so people could, "be the first to talk to the aliens."

(Yes, this directly contradicted the commonly-held assertion that certain powers-that-be were *already* talking to the aliens, and no, nobody minded the contradiction. Believing in two contrary facts at the same time was either more evidence that the entire planet had lost its mind, or it was just something human beings did sometimes.)

The devices were basically cheap one-way transmitters—walkie-talkies slaved to a dish that probably didn't work—that were in no way powerful enough to reach orbit.

Which was actually great. Every country on the planet was actively bombarding the spaceship with signals that *did* make it far enough, for basically the same reason ("be the first...!" etc.) and the last thing the ESS needed was more of that.

A DIFFERENT ALARM went off on the bridge. This one was much more important than anything being emitted by the craft projects on the ceiling.

Kris got back into the chair, and opened a channel to the rest of the team.

"*What Shuttle* incoming," she said. "Prepare for radio silence."

"We acknowledge," Josip said, from the shuttle.

"Hey, fellas," Davina said, to the tech bros, "you're gonna lose me for about a minute. Hang tight."

The *What Shuttle* was their shorthand for the Chinese-based shuttle that passed nearby on a fixed schedule. Whoever was inside that shuttle had been bombarding the alien ship with radio signals up and down the spectrum with great regularity for nearly two months. About half the time, the signal was close enough to the ESS team's channels to drown out their local communications, for about 90 seconds.

Ellis Aero, NASA, the U.S. government, the Europeans, and probably six or seven other corporate and government entities had asked China (nicely, and not-so-nicely) to Stop Doing That, and to work with the rest of the planet to establish communication with the aliens. Every request had been met the same response: What Shuttle?

For the moment, the ESS's solution was to keep track of when the shuttle would be nearby, and to observe temporary radio silence and suspend anything going on outside (if possible) until it passed.

Nobody knew if the *What Shuttle* had established communications, but it seemed doubtful. They were basically weaponizing the radio waves; it was hard to imagine they could *hear* anything said back to them. (What they were *saying* was, "Hello, and welcome to Earth" in Mandarin, which Kris personally found hilarious.)

They weren't even sure if there *was* a crew aboard. The *What Shuttle* was an older model, designed before a lot of the modern contrivances that allowed for crewless space travel, but there was no reason to think it *remained* a vessel requiring a crew. The Chinese could have gutted it and added automation. This seemed unlikely—it would have been cheaper to send up a drone that did exactly the same thing—but couldn't be dismissed out of hand. A couple of times, Dav tasked the ESS drone to a nearby orbit in an attempt to get a visual angle on the shuttle's windshield, but there was no way to get close enough to see anything unless they didn't want the drone back.

The *What Shuttle* wasn't the only incursion into local space they had to worry about; just the most annoying. As many as five other nations had gone the aforementioned cheaper option —send up a drone—with little success. This was contrary to an agreement brokered months ago between Ellis Aero, NASA, and the ESA, and agreed to (according to Max) by most of the nations on Earth. That agreement was: any attempts to communicate with and/or conduct research on the alien ship would go through the crew of the Ellis Space Station.

Only one of the five drones was still in orbit. One exploded before it made it high enough to establish a stable orbit, two fell apart after circling the planet a couple of times, and one was on its way to Jupiter. The fifth made it within about a half mile of the alien ship before falling into an orbit that was, for now, stable.

Nobody claimed credit for any of these. Monterrey did appear to know the origins of these wayward drones, but they weren't telling. Although Morris implied that the one in the stable orbit was from a private corporation and not a government entity, which was interesting, given Ellis was the only *known* corporate group with its own space program. But it was only a *little* interesting; the surviving drone was giving off no power signature. It appeared to be dead in space.

Assuming it didn't jump to life and adjust itself, the dead drone's orbit wouldn't be interfering with Sunset Station or the alien ship in anything less than five thousand years. Likewise, the debris fields from the two drones that fell apart posed no threat. But it was only a matter of time before things got crowded. Kris hoped they discovered something before it got to that point.

———

"KRIS, I'M ALL SET HERE," Paul said, shortly after the *What Shuttle* blackout ended.

"Roger that," she said. "Any luck?"

"If there's a seam here, I don't see it," he said.

"Come on back." She opened another channel. "Alan, how's it going over there?"

"Nearly done," he said.

"Any surprises?"

"Just another day in the coal mines. I'll be done in about ten."

"Roger that," she said.

Things were a bit awkward between her and Alan. Anyone who knew him well—which was everyone aboard the ESS— understood that as much as he was *capable* of being the commander, he had not been *prepared* for that responsibility in the moment. He did okay; nobody said otherwise. And once the situation became what it was, Kris did her level best to not over-step *too* much, make sure he was the last word on decisions and all that. His decision was, "let's ask Monterrey," *way* too often, but she tried not to let that get to her.

But Kris couldn't have been an easy person to be around, and she probably owed him a lengthy one-on-one to hash out any residual antipathy he might be carrying around. Just, not yet. There was too much going on.

A light flashed on the console. Someone in mission control wanted a word. She sighed, and opened the channel.

"Monterrey, this is Commander Standard. You rang?"

"Hi, Kris, it's Roman. How's things?"

"A little rain, but we're hoping for some clear skies later. Looking to get in a round of golf."

"Good, good," Roman said. Roman *had* a sense of humor, he just didn't want anyone to know about it. "Mr. Ellis is asking for a private convo."

"With me?"

"You're the star of the show."

"I think the *alien spaceship* is the star of the show, but okay. When?"

"He says now."

Kris looked down at the planet and did some quick math. "Isn't it like two in the morning in California?"

"You're assuming he's in California. Can I put him through?"

"Give me five minutes," she said. "Then patch him through to my private line."

"Roger that."

Kris opened a channel to the shuttle.

"Hey Jo, I have to step away. How are the boys?"

Josip had the shuttle near the back of the alien ship, at an angle that gave him line-of-sight on both Alan and Paul.

"No surprises," he said. "The little green men are on break."

"Very well. I have to step away. Dav will be in the cockpit if anything comes up."

She got up and touched Davina on the shoulder. Dav was still trying to explain how sound worked to the ground-based tech bros.

"Hold on, guys," Dav said, muting them. To Kris, she asked, "please, tell me there's an emergency."

"No such luck. I have to head in back; keep one eye on Josip for me?"

"Fine." Dav said. She looked down at her wristwatch and sighed. "Ten more minutes of this."

The watch was new. After discovering how perilous it was to live on a spaceship without a timepiece that remained accurate even during a power failure, Davina had an analog wristwatch sent up from the surface. It was reportedly *very* expensive, which was why she was the only one who got one.

"You can do it, babe," Kris said, as she pushed off and headed to her room.

———

THERE WERE ONLY three private bunk rooms in the hub, which meant they weren't exactly as private as all that. Like everything else associated with Ellis, "efficiency" was a big word; bigger than words like, "privacy," "decency," and "safety." "Efficiency" was the business-speak version of the word "cheap," which everybody understood but hardly anyone pointed out.

There were also three private bunk rooms in the bucket, which was how the math worked for a crew of six. Theoretically, only one team of three was supposed to be on active duty in the hub at a time. Sure, there might be crossover days here and there, but the bunks didn't take up a lot of space; the astronauts could double up when needed. (The bunks were also efficient, in that they were essentially sleeping bags in harnesses that could be lashed to any free wall in the hub.)

Currently, Alan and Josip were bunking together, Davina and Kris were bunking together, Paul got his own room (now doubling as the medical ward the designers also never factored into the design) and Sandee got the entire bucket to herself.

Kris slipped into the room she and Dav were sharing, closed the door flap, positioned herself in front of the video screen and slipped on a headset. Then she turned on the video, waited for a blinking light to go solid—this was an indication that the session to come would be private—and watched the screen jump to life.

In another minute, she was staring at Max Ellis. Based on the background, he was in London. (Or, he wanted her to think he was in London, for some reason known only to Max; these days, it was easy to drop a high-quality background on a video call.)

Max smiled. Something she learned about him almost immediately was that he was roughly twice as charming as he needed to be, considering how much he was worth. He'd somehow yet to become infected by the condition that turns the very wealthy into the weirdly unrelatable.

"Hello commander," he said. "How are you doing?"

"Why does everyone down there want to know how I'm doing today?"

"Just being polite."

"Well," she said, "I'm not doing fantastic, since you asked. My team hasn't had a Habitat break going on four months, and Alan's team isn't doing a lot better. We've got the discovery of a lifetime a few hundred yards away from us and we can't do anything except respond to photo requests, troubleshoot every-one's toys, and take meetings with hedge funders who think they're geniuses. Meanwhile, our computer expert is stuck in the bucket and down to one foot, which means we only have five able bodies doing the work of six, in a living space that sleeps three. If I took a vote today on whether we should keep going, or step outside without suits, I'm not sure how it would break. That's how I'm doing."

Max stopped smiling so much. "You're exaggerating."

"A little."

"Kris..."

"Yes, fine, it's not that bad," she admitted. "But it's not *fun* either. Tell me why you called."

"We ask a lot, I get it," he said.

"A *lot* a lot. Tell me why you called."

"Things are getting messy down here," he said.

"Um. In what way? And why don't you look unhappy about this? That sounds like bad news."

He nodded. "It's... not unexpected. Anticipated, actually. Just, well it all took longer than I expected, between you and me."

"Max, what are we talking about?" she asked.

"NASA and the ESA have a joint mission planned. It's an explicit violation of our agreement, so the *good* news is, very soon you can tear down all that shit they sent up. Cannibalize it for parts or, well, I don't really care what happens. It was all just sent there to waste our time anyway. Stalling until they got a go for their mission. Not sure anything does what they said."

"Are you...?" She bit her tongue, because she was now very much in the mood to tell the CEO to fuck off entirely. "What do you *mean*, waste our time?"

"This is better for us, politically. I know that seems like a small thing from your end, but before we went out there and did the *real* work, it had to look like we had no choice."

"You mean if something goes wrong, Max," she said. "If something goes wrong because of what *we* do, it had to look like there weren't any other reasonable options. You know, if the thing that goes wrong is the aliens blow up part of the planet, nobody's going to care about our political cover."

"I like the way I said it better."

"We can't have another team up here. I know it looks like we have a lot of room, but we really don't. Adding another ship full of tired people is an accident waiting to happen, and there aren't a lot of accidents up here that are non-deadly. You get what I'm saying?"

"I do, which is why I'm putting a stop to their plans."

This gave her pause. It was *possible* he was talking about publicly reaming them for going back on their agreement, or suing them, but she had a terrible feeling this was a different kind of threat. There was a decent chance the tech that was powering this joint NASA/ESA was Ellis tech. If some of it abruptly stopped working...

"Max," she said, "you're not going to hurt anyone, are you? I know a lot of those guys in NASA. I don't want them up here, but I also don't..."

"Oh, no, no, God no," he said. He knew exactly what she was implying, either because it actually was in the realm of the possible, or because Max Ellis's companies are routinely sued for exactly that kind of thing, frivolous accusation or not. "No, something like that would be catastrophic. Imagine the media blowback."

"I was thinking about the lives lost, but okay."

"That too. This'll be something else."

"Can you tell me what kind of something else?" she asked.

"Need you to trust me a little. It's getting handled; leave it at that. The upshot is, you and your team are going to be left alone. No new gadgets, no more *old* gadgets, and no other teams in your way. You'll be free to do whatever you think you need to do, in order to establish contact."

"Well that's *great*," she said. "And now I'm thinking this is actually bad news that sounds like good news. What's the other shoe?"

He leaned forward, marginally closer to the camera on his end, for emphasis. "You *have* to make contact," he said. "Whatever it takes."

"Sure, okay, but what if they don't want to just talk? My only weapons are a wrench, and body odor, and I'm not sure where the wrench is. Meanwhile, I don't know if they've even noticed we're here."

"Then figure out a way to make them notice."

This was so wildly in the other direction of every piece of instruction they'd been getting since day one, Kris really didn't know how to take it. Was there a *deadline?* What was going on here?

"When?" she asked. "Do we start, I mean."

"We'll let you know."

"And you can't tell me what you're going to do."

"It'll be handled," he said. "Oh, and I'm canceling all your media engagements. I want you a hundred percent concentrated on the EAS. Let Sandee know, would you?"

"Sure..." she said. And then he hung up, leaving her alone and *deeply* confused.

On the one hand, it was everything she wanted. On the other, there was only one reason for Max to *not* tell her what he was planning: he knew she wouldn't like it. But she lacked the right kind of sinister creativity to figure out what that could possibly add up to.

She pinged Sandee.

"Hey, Kris," Sandee said. The screen filled up with her vid feed from the bucket.

Sandee looked tired, and like she was in some pain, both of which was true. It was also true that the only people who *saw* this in her were aboard the ESS. Sandee had an entirely different game face she reserved for communications with the surface.

"Hi, got a minute?" Kris asked.

"I got seven, before my next thing. What's up?"

"Um, not sure. Are we... private?"

"Yes indeed."

The direct feed was assembled by Josip, whose actions were dictated by Sandee. Before this was done, communication between the two parts of the ESS was relayed to a satellite first, where it could also be listened in on by someone from the ground, should they desire to do so. This was done in the interest of greater privacy, at a time when seemingly the entire planet was interested in every single thing going on at Sunset Station. Monterrey didn't even know the private channels existed.

"Good," Kris said. "So, I just had a really peculiar conversation with Max Ellis."

"Yeah, I saw that private vid come up on my dash," she said. "They finally firing you?"

"Not exactly, no. He, um, he wanted you to know your calendar is getting cleared."

"Am *I* getting fired?"

"Nothing like that. Listen: how plugged in *are* we up here? To the internet, I mean."

Sandee grinned. "How plugged in do you want to be?"

"Something's about to happen down there," Kris said. "And I would *love* to know what."

"Tell me what you know," Sandee said, "and I'll see what I can do."

DAY ONE HUNDRED

NEWSBYTE

<u>*A hologram*</u>*! That's Dr. David Sorenstam's theory!*

"It isn't really there," says Dr. Sorenstam, of the Angstrom Institute. "What we're experiencing is some kind of optic effect that presents as a physical object. It's not a secret, either. The folks in space, they know it."

When asked who could accomplish a hologram this realistic, Dr. Sorenstam added, "Oh, it's definitely alien*; it's just not really there."*

Related:
** <u>How to make a hologram at home</u>*
** <u>Why everyone in Roswell is angry right now</u>*

NEWSBYTE

According to Margrit St. Germain, the secret White House-brokered agreement (reported exclusively by St. Germain last month in Variety) between Ellis Aerospace and NASA is falling apart!

"Word is, nobody's happy with the arrangement," St. Germain wrote, on her official Ellis Social account. "NASA thinks they can do better, and the Sunset Station team thinks NASA's wasting their time. Things are coming to a head."

Related:
** Top ten international treaties*
** Things you should ask your broker today*

MAX

"YOU'RE REALLY NOT GOING to tell me?" Margrit St. Germain asked. She seemed incredulous, which was one of her two default moods when engaging with Max. Margrit had a gift for pulling secrets out of people, which was why she was so good at her job. That the gift was at least 15% flirtation didn't change anything.

"You'll know soon enough," Max said. "Promise."

They were standing offstage, staring at an empty podium. Nina Lambo would be at the podium shortly, delivering a statement that would likely change the course of human history. The media pool on the other side of the room—which was only half-filled—had no idea.

The fact that the room was only half-filled was unsurprising; Nina had been pumping out anodyne updates for weeks, calling press conferences to announce discoveries that could have been made public in a two line press release. This had the effect of lowering everyone's expectations, regarding Nina capacity to disseminate newsworthy information, to the extent that if there was *any* buzz around her, it was buzz that her job may be at risk.

The tactic—of deliberately lowering expectations—was not how Max would have played this. He'd have rented out an airplane hangar and invited half the country. Nina went another way.

"It will be easier to accept if we look *surprised* by the news," Nina said. "Too much polish, and it'll seem like we're selling something."

"We *are* selling something," he told her.

"Yes, but they can't know that."

She was probably right, and since this was the kind of decision Max hired her to make, he didn't get in her way.

The closest he came to tipping his hand was in attending it himself (although the news media in the room didn't know this yet) and inviting Margrit.

It was his gift to her, for not using any part of their day-of-discovery phone call in a news story. Yes, she'd promised they were off the record, but there was enough grist in that conversation to float a half-dozen "unnamed sources…" teasers, or just a bunch of speculative public statements that somehow ended up being right.

Margrit wasn't seeing it as a gift.

"I'll know when *they* know, you mean," she said. "I don't think you understand what a *scoop* is, Max."

"Yes, at the same time as a bunch of stringers and interns. You'll be giving national media interviews while they're still trying to get their editors to pick up."

Then Nina stepped onto the stage from the opposite wing, and walked quickly to the podium.

Nina Lambo was an attractive, confident, intelligent woman whose look and manner was *always* on point, whether she was in front of the public or not. When she hurried across the stage a little *too* quickly, in a hairstyle that was just a *bit* unkempt and makeup that looked a little rushed, while carrying unsorted sheets of paper, a statement was being made even before she opened her mouth.

All of it was *theater*, but Nina was also a good actress.

Margrit took immediate notice, which was why she stopped accusing Max of wasting her time.

"*First contact?*" Margrit whispered.

"Good afternoon, everyone," Nina said, quieting the room. "I'm going to read from a prepared statement."

She paused to clear her throat before proceeding, which gave everyone who didn't already have a recording device out a chance to rectify that failing.

"At oh-nine-fourteen today, central standard time, the crew of the Ellis Space Station received a clear signal response from the alien ship. The signal was a tight beam transmission directed at one of the ESS's primary dishes, which itself was pointed at the alien ship. Based on the vector, signal strength, and content, our scientists consider the message to be genuine."

Nina paused again, just long enough for everyone to gasp, take a breath, and gasp again, but *not* long enough for anyone to shout out a question, as they were all a little stunned.

"We will be distributing the contents of the alien message with the press release, as soon as..."

She stopped for a beat; something on the paper in front of her had caught her eye.

It was difficult, perhaps, for the rest of the room to notice, but what happened next not only *appeared* unrehearsed, it actually *was* unrehearsed.

Nina covered the microphone with her hand, for what little good that did, as the room wasn't large enough to necessitate amplification anyway. "Hey, Bobby?" she said, to the intern at the edge of the stage. He had a pile of press release copies, which he was supposed to be distributing to the media as soon as Nina was done reading it out loud. "Hold back on that, okay?"

She uncovered the microphone. "We'll get you copies shortly," she said, to the press.

"What did the message say?" a woman in the second row shouted.

"Yes, Carol, thank you. The message is as follows: 'Hello to Sunset Station. Thank you for the welcome. We are here for peaceful reasons. Your planet is very noisy. We would speak to you, our nearest neighbors, only and alone. Quiet the sky and more will be heard.'"

She lowered the page, gave it a beat, and repeated, "'Quiet the sky, and more will be heard.' Ellis's linguistics department is looking over the text now, but it's our belief that the aliens have stated a preference to deal exclusively with our off-planet team. I'll take questions now."

Everyone in the room had a question, and they all decided to ask it at the same time, so the place went from pin-drop quiet to football stadium loud. Margrit, meanwhile, stepped away from Max and pulled out her phone. She would no doubt be scooping everyone in the room. Max, meanwhile, wanted to know what just went on between Nina and Bobby the intern.

Bobby was still at the edge of the stage, not knowing exactly what he was supposed to be doing, if not distributing copies.

"Hey!" Max hissed. He couldn't step out from the wing yet; in about two minutes Nina was going to be saying something to the effect of, "you know what, I can't answer that, but here's Max Ellis," and then it would be his turn. Before then, nobody was supposed to know he was there.

Bobby the intern didn't hear Max the first five times he hissed, but Nina had line of sight on both of them and could multitask. She directed Bobby backstage with a head nod.

"Oh, Mr. Ellis!" he said, as he too did not know Max was there. "It's exciting, isn't it?"

"Let me see the release," Max said.

"Oh, I'm not sure if I'm supposed to... Ms. Lambo..."

"I'll give it right back, son."

Reluctantly, Bobby handed one over.

"I need one of those too," Margrit said, from ten feet away, snapping her fingers.

"One sec, Marg," Max said, skimming the page.

There was something wrong with the text; specifically, the 'alien' message that Nina—and a small team of people who had been NDA'ed within an inch of their lives—spent weeks crafting. What was there wasn't what Nina recited at all, which was a real problem. *Nina's* version, recited by her from memory, was the correct one.

"Hello Sunset Station," the printed message began. "Thank you for the welcome. Danger. Danger. Danger. Danger. Danger. Danger. Danger. Danger. Danger. Danger."

It was some kind of corporate sabotage, possibly. But, a really weird one. Anyone with the access to do something like this could have done something a whole lot worse. That they didn't, made him more curious than angry.

Max shoved the page back into the intern's hand. "Bobby, is it?" he asked.

"Yes, Mr. Ellis."

"Bobby, I want you to find and destroy every last copy of this press release. Do you understand?"

"Not really, sir," he admitted.

"Max?" Margrit said, hand still outstretched.

"You'll get a copy later," Max said. To Bobby, he said, "Every copy. I'm not going to tell you why, but I *will* tell you that the future of this enterprise hangs in the balance."

Bobby looked like he was about to piss himself.

"Can I rely on you?" Max asked.

"Of—of course," the intern stammered.

"Go," Max said. "Hurry."

He ran off. When he crossed Margrit's eye line, she stared back at Max, silently asking what was wrong.

"Typo," he said. "You'll get a corrected copy. You know how it is when everything's last minute, Marg. First contact and all."

Margrit rolled her eyes and went back to her phone call.

Then Nina was calling him to the stage to take on some more question.

Max stepped out, to a murmur and slight applause. The press was decently subdued and/or stunned. It was hard to get a good read.

He passed Nina on his way to the microphone.

"You saw?" she asked.

"What the fuck was that?" he asked.

"I don't know," she said. "Someone's screwing with us. I'll get to the bottom of it."

"Find out who. If they work for me, fire them. If they don't, hire them."

"I will." She gripped his arm. "Now smile, Max; the world is watching."

He got behind the podium, smiled as instructed, and said, "all right, who has the question?"

DAY ONE HUNDRED
AND FIVE

NEWSBYTE

Aliens: they're just like us!

That's the word from the Ellis Alien Ship's PR team, according to their latest presser.

"They eat, and sleep, and breathe just like we do," says spokesperson Nina Lambo. But what *do they eat? What do they breathe? And just* where *did they come from?*

"We're working through a pretty huge language barrier," Lambo says, adding that the biggest communications breakthrough to date has been in the area of food recipes, of all things. "We'll ask those questions as soon as we figure out how. Meanwhile, they're excited to try chocolate!"

Related:

* *Ten sinful brownie recipes*
* *Best sci-fi aliens, ranked*
* *Poll: What should we call the aliens?*

—

NEWSBYTE

NASA and the European Space Agency scrap space flight plans!

In a World Entertainment Today exclusive, reporter Alvin DeCastro blows the lid off a top-secret joint mission that would have put a team in space as soon as next month!

"It was a done deal," writes DeCastro. "Up until the aliens broke their silence and scuttled the whole thing."

"A total fabrication," insists NASA director Laurence Bosco. "I don't know where they get these stories, but it's just not true."

Related:
* *Abduction survivor group sues aliens over mistreatment*
* *SETI faces funding shortfall*

SANDEE

"I CAN SEE YOU KRIS," Sandee said, from the cockpit of the ESS. "You look free and clear."

"Roger," Kris said. "Here we go."

The alien spaceship loomed large and nearby, and Kris Standard—who had just exited the airlock on the underside of the ESS—was on her way to its hull.

Davina, in a suit of her own, was down in the airlock, ready to back up Kris if she needed backup. Meanwhile, on the other side of the ship, Paul was in the shuttle, while Josip spacewalked nearby and Alan stood in the shuttle's airlock as support.

Everything about this setup was against established policy, from having as many as four—and potentially five, if Dav had to engage—away from the ESS at the same time, to the (unintentional) gender split.

(The latter was entirely because of the potential of bad optics, which wasn't something they had to worry about at the moment; nobody on the surface, outside of mission control, knew precisely what was going on, or if they did—if someone had a high-powered telescope pointed at them at the moment—

it wasn't actually possible to identify the gender of a person in a spacesuit.)

The plan was simple: Kris was going to touch the alien spaceship. Why? Because it was the only thing they hadn't tried yet.

IT HAD BEEN five days since Sandee's official role among the crew of the Ellis Space Station became effectively obsolete. That was because, five days ago and very abruptly, Sandee's direct contact with the surface was cut. She could still talk to Monterrey—everyone could—but the internet access she'd become accustomed to was gone.

Her primary gig was being the face of Sunset Station for the millions of Earthlings wanting to know about the day-to-day. There were a lot of good reasons to have a point person for media *in* space—the illusion of unfiltered information, a lack (or reduction of) mixed messages from different members of the crew, and so on—but the very best reason was that nobody else on the ESS took media engagement seriously enough to be any good at it.

And honestly? Fair. It was bullshit somewhere between 90-100% of the time. Internet opinions had no direct bearing on the crew's mission success, especially since their continued existence in space was thanks to private funding. (Unlike, say, NASA.) Anything they told the public was doled out as a *privilege,* and not an obligation.

Except it was more complicated than all that. The Ellis companies had a corporate reputation to uphold. The reputation of the vast majority of the Ellis empire was less-than-stellar, with Ellis Aero being a big exception. In a sense, the health of Ellis as a whole relied, at least partly, on how good everyone felt about Sunset Station, and how they felt about Sunset Station was largely governed by how well Sandee did her job.

Annnnd then her job went away.

Sandee always knew her connection to the rest of the world was mitigated (a nice word for "censored") by the ground crew at Ellis Aero. Nobody *told* her this, but it was pretty obvious: Q & A's came through with clumsy redactions; "live" interviews had inexplicable delays and strategic comms blackouts; emails landed with references to prior messages that had never been received; and so on. That didn't mean much to her until the day the pipeline to rest of the planet was shut down.

Well, *mostly* shut down They could get email. Heavily redacted, but they came through. This was to avoid any uproar regarding the ESS team being able to talk to their friends and family, and vice versa. It was a tiny hole that Sandee hadn't figured out how to exploit just yet. And that was something she'd been tasked with doing, because the other thing that happened five days ago was that the Sunset Station team was told, "do whatever you see fit, in order to establish contact with the alien ship." Without internet access—and unless or until Sandee figured out a way to hack the firewall—all she had was the emails.

Since their friends and family had no idea the ESS was unaware of current events, they had all kinds of questions, most of which didn't make it up. Some did, though. Franklin, a long-time friend of Sandee's, (who also happened to be a reporter for the New York Times, although it was possible the people running the censoring operation in Monterrey were unaware of this) sent up an email that was nearly empty of content, except for one sentence: *Chocolate: can you confirm?*

It was magnificently baffling. One day, she hoped to under-stand what it meant.

—

THE MOST JOYOUS moment for the crew, on the day they were told to make contact "no matter what," was removing all of the tacked on electronics that didn't belong to Ellis.

When not attached to the ceiling and walls of the hub, the equipment took up a lot of space; roughly the size of two additional humans, which was area they couldn't afford. But a *lot* of the stuff—or rather, the component parts, for cannibalizing—could prove useful at some future date, so jettisoning the entire bundle didn't seem sensible.

Fortunately, they had a perfectly good space platform that wasn't doing anything.

The electronics were catalogued—this meant taking some of it apart, which surely violated a couple of IP laws—and put into an unused shuttle crate. The crate had thick enough walls to hold atmosphere and enough radiation shielding to prevent anything short of a direct high energy cosmic ray from doing damage to the contents. All they had to do was attach magnets to one side and get it out there.

Once they'd taken care of that, they stopped the hab spin and brought Sandee up to the hub, which she *greatly* appreciated. She'd spent most of hundred-odd days since shattering her foot in the habitat, at 1G spin. This was to help the foot heal properly, at the possible expense of Sandee's long term mental health. She was pretty sure it didn't work, because her foot was still extremely fucked. Whether it was more or less fucked than it might have otherwise been, had she not lived in gravity for three months, seemed moot; fucked was fucked. It didn't come in degrees-of-fuckedness.

—

THE NOW-SUSPENDED efforts of NASA and the ESA to open lines of communications with the aliens produced *reams* of data. About half of it had been shared freely with Ellis Aerospace and the ESS team. Another quarter had been shared *un*willingly; many of the devices had open readouts that were easy to copy down before transmission to the surface.

The Sunset Station team had plenty to review, and thanks to whatever happened on Earth, they had all the time they wanted to review it (and there were teams in Monterrey who *had* been reviewing all of it, for quite a while) but the truth was, there wasn't *really* anything new there.

Radio signals made it through the hull; this they knew. There was no bounce-back or absorption going on. (They knew this, because they had indicators on the other side of the ship that registered the signal.) Light in the visible and non-visible spectrum bounced off the hull, as did low-level radiation, which indicated the ship had shielding. This was meaningful, inasmuch as it indicated the beings for whom the ship was built were, like humans, susceptible to radiation; perhaps *as* susceptible as humans.

There had been a lengthy discussion, among representatives from all the alphabet parties (EA, NASA, ESA) about bombarding the hull with higher levels of radiation, in order to check the absorption rate of the shielding. While all agreed that this would be useful information, if the alien hull wasn't up to the task, they may end up inadvertently hitting the ship's inhabitants with a lethal dose. Most agreed that this would not endear themselves to whoever was inside.

They had close-up images of the ship from every angle, knew its precise dimensions, and also knew that were the alien ship to be submerged in water, it would displace about 50,000 tons. This made it slightly larger than a Typhoon-class submarine.

There was plenty they didn't know, but they *knew* they didn't know it, and that was still something. For instance, they didn't know if the things sticking out of the lower portion of the front of the ship were guns. But multiple close-up images *suggested* they might be something else. (Antennas remained the best guess.) They also didn't know what kind of propulsion the ship used. But they could guess that whatever it was, it operated the way Earth rockets and shuttles did, i.e., by expelling something from the back.

Finally, they didn't know if there were any aliens inside.

If there were, why weren't they answering? Were they dead? Or—as Ellis's ground team thought—were they in stasis?

If there were *not*, what was the empty ship doing here? Was it a drone? What was the point of a drone the size of a Typhoon class submarine? Unless this was small for the creatures who built it? Except everything else about the ship's construction suggested it was built by beings who were human-sized, so that couldn't be it. Could it?

They also did not know what would happen if a physical object—a gloved human hand, say, or an extension from a drone—*touched* the hull of the ship.

That nobody had tried this yet seemed improbable, but there were absolute *hordes* of experts on the surface whose entire *raison d'etre* was teasing out ways in which well-intentioned people might act in a manner that could be perceived as an act of aggression. "Look, listen, speak to, but don't *touch*," was their motto.

These were the same experts who equated the use of a sighting laser on the hull with firing a shotgun, and thankfully, because of Sunset Station's newly granted freedom-to-do-whatever mandate, they no longer had to listen to that subset of experts.

▭

KRIS WAS ONLY ABOUT HALFWAY between the ESS and the alien ship when the alarm went off.

"*What Shuttle* coming," Sandee announced to the team, although they got the same alarm. "I've got eyes on you, Kris."

"I've got eyes on Jo," Paul said. "We're all standing by."

"Roger that," Sandee said. Then they lost all comms to a burst of static and distant Mandarin.

Frustratingly, the Chinese weren't part of whatever settlement had been reached on the ground, regarding the ESS's exclusive engagement with the aliens, so they still had to deal with the baffling passages of the *What Shuttle*. More than a couple of times, Sandee wished the alien ship *did* have guns pointed out of its nose; maybe it could shoot that damn thing.

(This was not a *nice* thought, inasmuch as the consensus was that there were people inside. She kept it to herself.)

The temporary loss of comms gave Sandee time to check in on the hack of the Monterrey firewall. She was trying a succession of keycode solutions with an automated program that assumed a code of six characters or less. This wasn't because she thought the encryption was of the six-characters-or-less variety; that was just the most the program could handle.

"Yeah, this ain't workin', Kris," she said to herself.

"*How can I help?*" Susie asked.

"Oh, hi, Susie. Don't suppose *you* have full internet access."

"*I don't understand! Do you have a question?*"

"I'm trying to get full internet access. Can you help?"

Susie was supposed to be the world's smartest artificial intelligence. She probably *was*, which didn't say anything good about the AI she was being compared to.

"*I'm not sure! Can you rephrase?*"

"It's okay," Sandee said. "Thanks for asking."

"*Of course!*" Susie said.

The *What Shuttle* interference ended a few seconds later. Sandee pinged everyone's comms to make sure all was well.

"You're a go to continue," she said.

"Proceeding," Kris said.

A light flashed on her dashboard, indicating Monterrey wanted a word. Hopefully not about Sandee's attack on the firewall, which she hoped was going unnoticed.

She opened the channel. "Go, Monterrey," she said.

"Need an update," Morris said, not wasting any time with niceties.

The mandate to allow the ESS team to follow their bliss, as regarding the alien craft, had not gone over well with a decent portion of the support team, and they weren't pulling punches about it. She thought their biggest problem (which they seemed unable to articulate) was the loss of veto power. Kris pretty much did whatever she felt like a lot of the time anyway, but now that approach was sanctioned, and they hated it.

"Kris is a few minutes out," Sandee said.

"We're deaf and blind down here," he said.

That's because I'm not sending it to you, she thought. "Hang on, lemme check that."

Sandee switched channels. "Team, Monterrey's eyes and ears are up," she said. "Act accordingly."

"If we have to," Kris said.

"Roger that," Alan said.

Jo, Paul and Davina acknowledged with annoyed grunts of their own. After the past few months, the team very much liked not having Monterrey in their ear at all hours. Even Alan.

Sandee flipped the appropriate switches, and opened the channel with the ground.

"How's that, Mo?" she asked.

"We've got you now, thanks," he said. "What was the problem?"

"Nothing's been quite the same since the power failure. You know how it is."

KRIS

AFTER THE PASSAGE of the *What Shuttle*, it took Kris another half an hour of slow-drifting before she was close enough to touch the alien hull.

The slowness of her approach was probably unnecessary; today would not be the first time one of them had gotten this close. But since the *intent* here was to make contact, approaching it as one might approach a wounded lion seemed valid.

"Anyone know any prayers?" Kris asked.

"*Here is a list of the top prayers, sorted by denomination!*" Susie enthused.

"Not you, asshat. Shut up."

"*Of course!*"

"Do you *want* a prayer?" Sandee asked.

"Susie ruined the moment," Kris said. "Never mind."

Kris reached out, and, after a deep breath, put her hand on the ship.

It was incredibly anticlimactic. The alien spaceship was, A: solid, and, B: did not kill her instantly. While she was very happy about the not-dying, overall this qualified as a net-zero in terms of new things learned.

She took her hand away.

"Anything?" she asked. "Sandee?"

"No change that I can see," Sandee said.

"Paul?"

"Nothing here," he said.

"How did it feel?" Davina asked.

Dav was in the hub airlock, ready to launch herself into space if needed, which unfortunately meant she had nothing to look at in there, other than what she could see with her naked eye through the airlock porthole. Under different circumstances, Kris would have had Dav in the cockpit and Sandee in the suit. But Sandee was unlikely to be cleared for spacewalk until her foot healed, and her foot was never going to heal. Kris didn't know this for sure; nobody did. But it seemed pretty obviously true, if only from the pained expression on Sandee's face every time she moved.

"You mean, did an electrical current move through me?" Kris asked. "Did I hear angels singing? Did my ancestors appear in a vision?"

"Yes, anything like that," Dav said.

"Nope."

"Pity."

"I'm going to try something," Kris said. "Hang on."

With a little maneuvering, Kris got herself turned around; now her boots were facing the ship. She pushed closer, and made contact.

She heard a gentle click, when the magnets engaged with the hull.

"I can walk on it, guys," she said.

This seemed like another unimportant discovery, but it was actually decently relevant. None of the tests conducted on the ship had firmly established what the hull was made of, because nobody was willing to sign off on directly testing it. (To *really* know what it was made of, they would have had to remove a portion of the hull, and that was obviously out of the question.) The belief was that the outside was made of a metal alloy, but what those metals were, how much of the alloy was metal, and how much of that metal was the kind one could attach a magnet to? These were all unknowns.

Kris started a slow walk along the side of the ship, toward the nose.

"Still no change," Sandee said.

"Should I try that over here as well?" Josip asked.

"Let's see if the footsteps wake up anybody first," Kris said.

"You should have brought a hammer," Davina suggested. "That would definitely wake someone up."

"The hammer is day two, maybe," Kris said. "Let's survive day one first."

"I probably shouldn't have to say this," Morris said. "But no hammers, please."

"Well now we're *definitely* trying that," Kris said.

"Guys, hey," Paul said. "I think I may have something. Sandee, switch to infrared."

"Will-do," she said. And then, "Oh. Huh. That's new."

"What is it?" Kris asked.

"Cascading light pattern," she said. "You, um, I think you need to disengage and come on back."

"Is it bad?"

"I don't think it's good or bad, but I don't know what it *is*. We may need some more eyes on this."

IT TOOK Kris over an hour to get back to the hub, and it was another two before Paul, Alan and Josip were back inside, and another hour after *that* before the six of them were on the bridge together, looking at what Sandee and Dav had already reviewed a hundred times.

Monterrey was still on the live feed, in case they had something interesting to offer.

"We think it's safe to say, you woke up something in the ship," Morris said.

"That's the extent of your analysis?" Kris asked.

"That's the *start* of our analysis," Mo said. "We think it may be a language, but our access to linguists is limited right now."

"Is it really?" Sandee asked. "Why is that?"

"*Linguistics is the study of—*" Susie began.

"Shut up, asshat," Kris said.

"*Of course.*"

"It just is," Morris said.

This led to an awkward pause. Everyone aboard the ESS was well aware they weren't being told *something*, and nobody was remotely comfortable with that fact. But this wasn't the time to relitigate that particular concern, not when they'd finally gotten the alien ship to do a trick that didn't involve causing a power failure.

"Loop it again," Kris said to Sandee, who remained at the helm of the cockpit.

"Sure," Sandee said. She backed up the image on the main screen and ran it through, for all to see.

What they were looking at was Kris, in her suit, walking along the side of the ship. In this first play-through, there was nothing of note. Then it ran again, only with an infrared filter. *This* time, each step triggered cascading whorls of light along the hull. It was a little like the circlets created by a stone dropped in a pond, except instead of impact waves, they were seeing random curlicues. Every now and then the free-roaming curls collided and bounced away from one another.

The random whorls continued as long as Kris was touching the ship. Once she detached, the lightshow stopped.

Sandee backed it up and ran it again.

"Not sure I want to wait for a linguist, Mo," Kris said, as it played.

"It could be important," Morris said. "We advise you not proceed until we've conducted a thorough analysis."

But this was meant for us, she thought. There was no reason to think any such thing, but it seemed right anyway.

"Kris, I don't think we *have* a way forward," Alan said. "Might be a good idea to wait."

"Screensaver," Sandee muttered.

"What?" Kris asked.

"Sorry, I just figured out what this reminded me of. These could be words, but that doesn't mean they're a message. I think the *pattern* is a message."

"Then we still need a linguist," Morris said.

"Wait, wait," Paul said. "I think I saw something. Pause it."

Sandee did. Paul floated to the console.

"Can I?" he asked.

Sandee made a hands-off gesture and kicked away from the console, floating backwards. Kris noted, again, the pain Sandee was trying hard not to show.

We should have made you rotate out, she thought. But Sandee had insisted, and it was more convenient to everyone that she not, and so here they were.

Paul got his hands on the video controls. He wasn't as proficient as most, so it took a minute, but he found the spot he was looking for, paused it, and said, "Okay, look over there on the left."

"Yes, yes, I see it," Josip said. "Close up on that sector. There is a dead space."

Paul adjusted the image to focus on a section of the ship about one-third away from the nose, where none of the infrared curlicues were visiting.

"Back it up and rerun it," Kris said. "Keep the closeup, normal speed."

Paul backed it up and played it through. Then he did it a couple more times to make sure they weren't talking themselves into seeing something that wasn't there. But it *was* there: a roughly square-shaped section of the hull that was immune to the lights cascading all around it.

"Could that be an error on our end?" Kris asked. "Like a missing pixel?"

"I don't see how," Davina said. "The lights aren't passing through the squared space; they're bouncing off. The ship clearly thinks it's there."

"What've you got?" Morris asked.

"I think we found the door, Mo," Kris said.

▭

"WE WERE GOING to have to cut our way into the ship eventually," Josip said. "Now we know where."

Josip was pragmatic, in a slice-through-the-bullshit kind of way, that made him good at what he did. It also made him a little obstinate.

"Yes of course," Sandee said. "Let's do that; nothing says, 'hello, we are a friend,' like exposing their ship to the vacuum of space."

"You don't know that," he said. "Their ship could have sealable compartments."

"Ours doesn't," she said.

"*Ours* is not the size of a nuclear submarine," he countered. "And we *do*, provided one breaches us at the airlock."

"The square is a door," Paul said. "Right? We're thinking it's a door?"

"Or a hatch, or a maintenance panel, or a place where they patched their hull with different material," Davina said. "All we really know is that it's a square."

Paul turned to Kris. "*You* think it's a door," he said.

"I do, yes."

"Monterrey doesn't think so," Alan said.

This was true. Shortly after clarifying the image of the squared space, Sandee sent it down to Monterrey. Morris, on review, rather stridently insisted that sometimes a square is just a square, and they needed more information before doing anything about the square, and everyone at Sunset Station needed to stand down until the opinion-makers on the surface formulated an opinion. It was at that point that Kris had Sandee cut the line to Monterrey.

"We don't need their input to make a decision," Kris said. "But I'd like it if *we* were in agreement about what to do next."

"Agreement?" Alan repeated. He said it like it was a curse word. "Why start now? You're going to decide what you decide."

"Alan, that's unfair," Davina said.

"I'm just saying this is not a democracy, so let's not pretend it is. Commander Standard, what do *you* want us to do?"

She sighed; this was not how she wanted this meeting to go.

Kris never did find time to talk to Alan about how the whole command thing had been handled, and now she was paying for it.

She took a deep breath and waited to see if anyone else wanted to take a shot—he was not the only one with complaints, and *everyone* was tired—before continuing.

"Uh, all right," Kris said. "What do we know about the aliens so far?"

"Nothing," Davina said.

"*How can I help?*" Susie asked.

"Not now, asshat," Kris said.

"*Of course!*" Susie said.

"I'll rephrase," Kris said. "What do we *think* we know?"

"We think they're probably about our size," Paul said.

"Yes," Josip agreed, "the rivets in the hull indicate a comparable hand size, and tool size. If that is a hatch, it is a hatch meant for beings our approximate size."

"Their vision works differently than ours does," Sandee said.

"How so?" Kris asked.

"Infrared," she said. "The lights on the outside of the hull; it makes no sense to put that on a ship if you can't see it without a special filter. Therefore, their vision is based on a different range of the light spectrum than ours."

"Did any of the tests from before look at infrared?" Paul asked.

"Yes," Davina said. "I reviewed the light spectrum data collected both by us and NASA. Nothing notable was found at the time, in the non-visible ranges. Either they simply weren't looking at the right moment, or..."

"Or they had to be looking when someone was in contact with the hull," Kris finished.

"Yes."

"*How can I help?*" Susie asked, again.

"Asshat..." Kris said.

"We need to open the door on the alien ship," Davina said, to Susie. "Can you help with that?"

"*We need the door open,*" Susie repeated.

"That's right," Davina said. "Can you help?"

"I don't know!" Susie said. *"Here is more about doors!"*

"That's enough, Susie, thanks for trying," Kris said. To rest of the room, she asked, "what else do we know about the aliens?"

"Well, there's the obvious stuff," Alan said. "They can't survive in space without protection, they can't travel *through* space without some kind of mechanical propulsion..."

"They are more advanced than we are," Josip said.

"Are we sure of that?" Kris asked.

"We can be reasonably certain the ship came from outside our solar system, because if there was a species *in* our system capable of space flight we'd have known this already. We are not capable of building a ship that can travel such distances. Therefore, yes; I believe we are sure of that."

"They don't want to talk to us," Sandee said. "We know that too."

"Which doesn't make any sense," Paul said. "Why come all this way, park in orbit, and not say something?"

"Any number of reasons," Kris said. "They could be in suspended animation. Or, they may just experience time differently than we do in some fundamental way, and this isn't long for them. Or, they may have come here not realizing someone on the planet is sufficiently advanced to *notice* them in space."

"They parked next to us," Davina reminded her. "They must know we're here."

"True that they parked next to us. Not necessarily true that they know we're here. If we assume they can see infrared, can we also assume they can see *us?*"

"Again, we have to believe they are like us in certain fundamental ways," Josip said, "based on the starship they constructed. That is not the vessel one uses if one is an intelligent amoeba-like entity that views time in eons and is blind to the visible spectrum."

"I know we've just spent the past few months on this," Alan said, "but what if they *have* tried to communicate and we just can't figure out how? Maybe by way of a channel humans haven't discovered yet?"

"I offer the same answer," Josip said. "That ship is advanced, but it is not *that* advanced."

"*How can I help?*" Susie asked.

"Honest to God, I'm going to unplug her if this keeps up," Kris said.

"Still trying to open the door," Davina said.

"*Of course!*" Susie said.

"I don't even hear her anymore," Davina said.

"She's better than she used to be," Sandee said.

"Annoying and useless is still annoying and useless," Kris said. "And now we're talking about her instead of—"

"*The door is open,*" Susie said.

They all stopped talking to stare at one another, and then "up," at Susie. (For reasons nobody could quite explain, disembodied voices to humans were always "up.")

"What did you say?" Kris asked.

"*The door is open,*" Susie repeated.

"Um, Susie? Which door?" Davina asked.

"She can't open doors, can she?" Paul asked, under his breath. "On a spaceship? That would be bad, right? We all agree on that?"

"*The door is open,*" she said, again.

"Davina, can you bring up that region of the ship, on the monitor?" Kris asked. "The live feed?"

Dav called up the camera that kept an eye on the alien ship, and zoomed in on the appropriate section of the hull. The squared off space they could only previously identify in a still shot of the ship's infrared signature was now easy to pinpoint; that part of the hull now appeared to be missing.

They stared in mute shock, as Davina zoomed in closer still. There was nothing to see on the other side, but the "door," as Susie put it, was "open."

"Well, that's creepy as hell," Alan said.

"Susie must have been monitoring the external feed for us," Sandee said. "I told you, she's not as bad at this as she used to be."

"Is that right, Susie?" Kris asked. "Were you monitoring the alien ship for us?"

Susie said, *"an adult monitor lizard can grow up to..."*

"And she's back," Kris said.

"That's enough, Susie," Davina said. "Thank you."

"Of course!"

DAY ONE HUNDRED AND SEVEN

NEWSBYTE

President Malden to Max Ellis: I want to talk to the aliens!

Max Ellis to President Malden: no!

"Look, all questions to or about the aliens should be directed to the EAS PR team," Ellis said. "No disrespect intended, but let's make sure an apple is an apple, and a screwdriver is a screwdriver before we start making introductions to world leaders. That's all I'm saying."

But if President Malden insists? "He should talk to Nina Lambo," Ellis said. "That's what she's there for."

Related:
** <u>Ancient wars that could have been prevented if they had phones</u>*

* _The Rosetta Stone's secrets, unlocked_

KRIS

IT WAS A REAL HOLE. That was the first thing they confirmed, before making plans to check it out up close. They did this by firing another laser at it from the drone. The laser didn't bounce back at the hull, but it *did* come back after hitting a wall inside, which also told them the cavity was eleven meters deep. They took this to mean the open door wasn't exposing the entire interior of the alien ship to space, a not-entirely-supported assumption they made anyway. (They also assumed it was an airlock, which assumed there was atmosphere inside, which assumed the aliens breathed, and so on.)

From the planning, to the moment when Kris was actually outside and poised at the edge of the opening, it took twelve hours. This included mandatory naps for everyone, because no matter how exciting all of this was, they were also human beings, and human beings needed sleep or they made mistakes, and mistakes were bad. It was likely none of them actually *slept*, seeing as they were on the verge of (hopefully) making alien contact, but they at least *rested*.

Kris definitely didn't sleep. She spent her time in the sleeping bag second-guessing everything that had led up to this point, including the part where she insisted she be the one to go inside. She wanted to believe it was so she didn't risk anyone else's life unnecessarily, but not only was that not the truth, she didn't think anyone else on the ESS thought for one second that it might be the truth.

It *was* true that if she told, say, Paul to go in first, and Paul didn't come back out alive, Kris would spend however much time she had left kicking herself for putting him in that position. But she'd have felt that way no matter what she happened to ask Paul (or anyone else) to do; basically, everything in space was potentially fatal, and every assignment had some degree of risk. There would be self-kicking in her future regardless.

Anyway, she was going to be the first one in and that was that.

She left for the alien ship from the ESS's airlock, along with Alan, to whom she would be tethered while she went inside. Davina and Josip were in the shuttle, with Josip as backup. That left Sandee and Paul in the hub to keep Monterrey updated (they weren't going to have Morris in Kris's head on this mission, because Morris was freaking out) and to tell Susie to shut up whenever that was appropriate.

Kris fixated on the open door for the entire journey across the open space between the ESS and the alien ship, half expecting it to close abruptly before she had a chance to get there. (This fear, which had become almost overwhelming during the planning stages, was another reason she didn't get any sleep.) It made her want to hurry which, again, was a bad thing to do in outer space.

Once they reached the ship, she and Alan positioned themselves on either side of the opening, with the tether crossing the space between.

Alan peered over the lip. "Looks dark in there," he said.

Kris lit a flashlight and shined it inside. No aliens waiting to pounce, or bears, or anything else except walls.

The second thing they went about confirming, before they planned this adventure, was that the dark hole in the side of the ship—having been proven a hole—was actually *dark*, by looking at it through the infrared filter. It was. Now, up close, Kris popped a function on her helmet that dropped the same filter over her view, turned off the flashlight, and checked again.

"Still dark," she said.

"Did you see an inner airlock door?" Alan asked.

She relit the flashlight and probed again. It was a tight, directed beam that was less than ideal when it came to revealing all the corners of an eleven-meter-deep room, but she gave it her best.

"I'm not seeing one," she said. "But there *has* to be, right? What's the point otherwise?"

"To catch someone stupid enough to go in," he said. "I don't know, but tell me how this makes sense. Aliens show up in orbit, don't say *anything* for three and a half months, then open a door and expect us to just go inside. Why don't they come *out?*"

"Do you see any immediate threats, Alan?" Kris asked. "Because I don't. I get you, but the only way to make sense of it is to keep going. The answers are in there somewhere. Sandee?"

"I'm here," Sandee said.

"Tell the ground I'm going in."

"Roger that."

Kris turned the light off, put both hands on the tether, nodded to Alan—who braced himself—and then floated over the opening, gave her attitude thrusters a nudge, and crossed the threshold.

Rather abruptly, she was sucked into one of the walls, face first. More alarming than painful, she let out a scream.

Alan, on the other end of the tether, shouted, "Are you okay?" and "I'm pulling you back, I'm pulling you back!"

"No," Kris coughed. "I'm okay."

She tried to stand, decided against it, and rolled over instead, onto her back.

"Kris, your heartrate just spiked," Sandee said. "You all right?"

Kris looked down at the hole she'd come in through. The wall she was on was the one that ran parallel to the bottom of the ship. It wasn't a *wall* at all; it was the floor.

"This ship has gravity," she said. "It was kind of a surprise."

She could barely move and barely breathe, but had no idea if this was because the gravity on this ship was greater than Earth-equivalent, the same, or less. It had been so long since she'd been subjected to it, she simply couldn't tell.

With a tremendous effort, she got up onto her elbows.

"Your vitals are all over the place," Sandee said, with some urgency. "Maybe Alan *should* pull you out."

"No, it's okay. This really fucking sucks, but it's not... I can get used to it. I just need to find my feet."

"*How can I help?*" Susie asked.

"Shut up, Susie," Kris muttered.

"*Of course!*"

Kris pulled her legs under her and, using one of the walls for support, managed to stand. Then she remained still for a solid ten-count, to make sure she didn't fall over again.

It was too much weight. She was going to have to get lighter if she wanted to move.

"Guys, I'm gonna remove my booster lattice," she said.

"Kris, you shouldn't do that," Alan said.

"I agree with him," Davina said. "Come back out and we'll work on a solution."

"Like what, Dav?" Kris said. "It's not like there's a lighter suit for me to change into."

"When we return, it will be with the G-meter," Josip said.

This wasn't a terrible idea. The G-meter was a compact version of a bathroom scale, combined with a five ounce flat of iron. They used it to tune the rate of the bucket's spin to match Earth's gravity. Very simply, once the scale said the iron weighed five ounces, they were in tune. If they were to put it on the floor of the alien ship, and suddenly the five ounce iron flat weighed *more*... Kris would know she wasn't overreacting.

"We should definitely do that," Kris said. "Next time. But I'm still removing the lattice."

"Kris..." Dav said.

"No, look, Alan still has his boosters and the shuttle is right behind him. If I gotta leave fast, someone should be able to reach me."

"Sure, unless we lose power again," Sandee said.

"If we lose power, the booster lattice won't do me any good anyway," Kris said. "Guys, I'm already half out of it, and I'm standing in fucking *gravity*. I'm not gonna float off. Let me recon at least *one* room today, huh?"

"You're being reckless, dear," Davina said. "But we are hardly in a position to stop you."

Kris didn't think she was being reckless, but it was possible Max's admonition to do "whatever it takes" to make first contact was a larger part of Kris's risk decision tree than she was readily acknowledging.

"I'm proceeding," she said, sliding the lattice off her back. It fell to the floor, silently. An alarm went off in her helmet, signaling news of the uncoupling, which was evidently bad. But she could stand up straight now, which was *not* bad.

"All kinds of alarms coming from the suit," Sandee said.

"Yeah, hang on," Kris said, silencing them. "Better?"

"Better. Monterrey just had a stroke, but better."

"I am continuing to the back of the room."

She turned the flashlight on again, and began a slower, more thorough trace of the walls. There were a couple of things of note, neither being a door: the ceiling had small insets that looked like vents; there was a raised panel on the wall opposite the open airlock.

"Got something that looks like a control panel," she said. "Heading there."

One of the things they taught in astronaut training, when she was at NASA, was how to maneuver in a bulky spacesuit in (near) weightless conditions. The class was conducted in a water tank, which they got to the bottom of by attaching their boots to weights. The part where she had to walk in the suit, weights on, across the room to the water tank, was exactly how trying to cross the airlock felt now.

She got within five feet of the panel, and then had to stop; the tether between her and Alan wasn't long enough. "I need to unhook," she said. "I can't reach the far wall."

"You won't do any such thing," Alan said. "We can get a longer tether."

"That'll take as long as the G-meter," she said.

"Kris, again, we don't have to do this all in one day."

He was not only right, he was right in the same way Kris would be right if it was him inside and her outside. It was the right command decision.

But the panel was right there.

"I'll stay tethered if you come inside," she said.

"That's not the right protocol," Davina said. "Alan, you should stay where you are."

"If he stands on the inside of the door, I'll have enough rope and you guys can still see him. Okay?"

"I think that's a bad idea," Paul said.

"We're standing on a fucking mountain of bad ideas, Paul," Kris said. "I just need Alan to take a few steps."

"And if you're both overcome by the gravity?" Paul asked.

"The gravity doesn't kick in until about two meters past the doorway," she said. "He should be fine. Alan? What do you think?"

"Yeah, I'll do it," Alan said. "But then you're getting out. Give me a second."

He had to crouch to fit into the doorway, because—unlike the room itself, which had a high ceiling—the square opening wasn't large enough to stand up in.

"How's this?" he asked, leaning forward to get the tether attached to his waist as close to her as he could.

"That'll work. Did you hit gravity?"

"No, I'm okay."

"Kris, mission control is saying you guys should get out of there," Sandee said.

"Any reason other than they're a bunch of grandmas?" Kris asked.

"Nothing specific."

"Okay then. Tell them we'll be right out."

Kris took another three steps forward, and then she was in reach of the raised panel. After looking at it from a couple of angles, she was able to confirm that it was, indeed, raised and not an illusion of the meager light. It was a difference of only about a quarter of an inch, but that seemed huge given the rest of the wall was smooth.

She put her hand on the panel. As much as she could tell through the heavy glove, the surface was smooth; there were no bumps or indents indicating function.

"Hey, Kris," Davina said, from the shuttle, at an angle that could see partway into the room. "IR filter just went nuts."

"Noted," she said. She dropped the infrared screen on her helmet and... there it was.

The room was lit up, with rows of curlicue scribbles running parallel along the floor, ceiling and walls. "Sandee, I think you were right; these guys can see infrared. They also hate straight lines."

"Perhaps when you meet one you can ask it why," Josip said.

Alan, at the edge of the room, had pulled down his helmet screen too. "When we saw this on the hull I took it as writing," he said.

"If it is, it's saying the same thing over and over," Kris said.

"Hey, at what point is it officially weird that we *haven't* met an alien?" Davina asked. "They must know we're inside by now, right?"

"That's a good question," Kris said.

She turned back to look at the panel. It was also lit up, but with smaller scribbles with more variability. *Now* that *looks like writing*, she thought.

There were three circles underneath the writing. What she should have been doing next, was taking a photo of the panel, sending it back to the ESS, and leaving. They'd already learned more about the spaceship in the past two hours than they'd learned in the previous three months; it would make sense to stop here and review all they had. She'd seen the room, confirmed there were no aliens, and had a basic plan. As the others had been imploring her to remember, slow and steady was a basic rule of space exploration, and that held even when she was technically indoors.

What was *not* a basic rule of space exploration, but felt like it should be, was: if you don't know what the button does, don't push the button. (This may actually have been a horror movie rule, but it felt applicable in this situation.) This was a problem for her, because the middle of the three circles happened to be pulsing gently, the universal symbol for, "Hello, I am a button, please push me," and she really very much wanted to find out what happened if she did that.

"All right, we got what we came for," Alan said. He gave the tether a gentle tug. "Let's get out of here."

"Yes," she agreed. "Just a second."

But what if the airlock door closes behind us, she thought, *and we never get this close again? What if I never get to push this button?*

Kris was not a particularly religious person, having been raised lapsed Catholic, but she knew perfectly well that this was the Devil's voice. That didn't mean the Devil was wrong.

"Kris?" Alan asked.

"Yeah. Sorry. I gotta try something."

She reached out, extended one finger, and pushed the button.

Immediately, the lights along the walls started flashing, in a cascade directed toward the inner wall. There was no sound to hear—it being the vacuum of space and all—but it *felt* like some sort of alarm was going off, as a warning for what was about to happen.

What happened next certainly warranted alarm bells. First, Alan discovered where the door to the airlock had gone, because it reappeared at his feet, rising up from the floor slowly enough for him to scramble. Instinctively, he went *backwards*, away from the center of the room and—importantly—away from Kris.

"Kris, get out of there!" Alan shouted.

She turned around to see her escape route already half cut off by the rising door.

"I'm coming!" she said, but there was the problem with the gravity, which made moving rapidly a practical impossibility. Alan pulled as hard has he could on the tether to help drag Kris to the exit, but all this did was cause her to lose her balance. She fell face-first on the floor.

By the time she looked up again, the door was almost completely closed. There was still about an inch of space between the ceiling and the top of the door, because the tether was preventing it from forming a seal, but since she couldn't fit through a one inch gap, it didn't do her much good.

"Kris, Kris are you okay?" Alan shouted.

"I'm okay, are you?" she asked.

"Did you do that?"

"I might have, yeah. I'll, I can fix this. I just have to…"

Then something violent happened. The problem was, the door wasn't flush with the hull; it had risen up through the floor at a spot about two feet from the opening. Evidently, closing the airlock was a two-step process. Step one, the door came up. Step two, it slid *outward* and completed the seal.

Step two sucked. It happened so fast, it jerked Kris—halfway standing, still tethered—off her feet again, this time landing hard on her back with such force that she got to see some entirely unwelcome bright colors at the edge of her vision.

She didn't know what happened to Alan on the other side, but imagined the door probably hit him pretty hard. Was he hurt? Did he break a leg? Was his suit damaged? She tried to ask, but nothing sensible came out.

Then the end of the tether—coiled steel that was supposed to be impossible to cut—hit her in the face.

Oh, she thought, *is that a crack?*

Then she blacked out.

SANDEE

ALAN SCREAMED in pain when the door snapped the unbreakable tether and sent him flying backwards and away from the alien ship. Now he was tumbling end-over-end, and not answering any hails.

"Sandee, what's happening up there?" Morris was asking.

"Can't talk," Sandee said, muting their connection. "Davina?"

"We got him," Dav said, nudging the shuttle into an intercept with Alan. Already, the shuttle airlock door was opening, with Josip ready to go.

"Be careful," Paul said. Paul had adjusted one of the hub's cameras to focus on Alan, as much as that was possible. (They were not fantastic at tracking moving objects.) "Suit looks intact, but I think his arm may be broken."

"Does anyone have eyes on Kris?" Davina asked.

"Concentrate on getting me to Alan, please," Jo said.

"Fuck you, I can do both," Dav said. "Anyone?"

"She's inside the ship," Sandee said. She still had a half-dozen cameras pointing at the alien hull, which looked as impregnable as it had before the door opened. "I'm trying to reach her."

Sandee's board was getting a clear signal of Kris's vitals, which meant both that a signal could get out from the other side of the hull, and Kris wasn't dead. They were stable, which was good. Her *suit* was sending back a breach warning, which was very much not good, but Sandee didn't want to tell Davina about that while Dav was busy rescuing Alan.

"Kris, can you hear me?" Sandee asked, on a private channel. "Kris, come in."

She wasn't answering. Sandee checked Kris's video feed to see if that could tell her anything, but it was delivering an error; either her camera had been damaged, or Kris had deactivated it.

The breach warning indicated a slow leak. An alarm should be going off in Kris's helmet that would be really difficult to ignore if she was conscious.

"Paul, look at this readout," Sandee said. "Is this, like, *too* calm?"

He floated over and looked. "Yeah, she's out cold," he said. "And that alarm..."

"I know," Sandee said. "I don't know what to do about any of it."

"From here? Nothing we can do right now except hope she wakes up and patches that leak. If she's not awake in another hour, we may have to send Josip out there with a torch."

Outside, Davina had the shuttle next to the tumbling Alan. Jo exited the airlock.

Sandee opened the comms to the shuttle team. "Hey, watch that tether," she said.

Part of the cord was still attached to Alan's belt; the other end was spinning around with him. It didn't look like much, but if it hit Josip in the wrong place, there would be consequences.

"I am aware," Jo said.

"Arm's definitely broken," Paul said, either to himself or to Sandee. Not on comms, either way. "Concussion, too, unless his mic is dead..." He looked at Sandee. "I need to prep; you okay here?"

"Go," she said, which seemed unnecessary as he was in the process of leaving the bridge already.

"Tell me when Kris wakes up," he said, leaving.

"Sandee," Davina said. "Kris. Tell me."

"She's alive, but we think she's unconscious," Sandee said.

"You think E.T. dosed her?"

"I..."

"I'm kidding," Dav said. "Sort of."

"Stay on task with Alan, Davina," Sandee said.

"Yes, yes."

A noise that might be described as an angry notification was sounding off from the communications panel. It was Monterrey, demanding an update. They were also probably wondering why they couldn't force their way back into the ESS's systems to see what was happening for themselves.

There *had* been, up until very recently, a way for ground control to take remote command of the ESS. It was called the Puppet Show directive, and in the most extreme of examples, it could be considered a safety measure—like, if the entire crew was disabled for some reason. (Non-trivially, and obviously, it only worked if Sunset Station had *power*; it was just as useless a failsafe as everything else that day.) It also gave them access to all the video and audio outputs on the ship, which—again, in the *extreme*—would be important in ascertaining what was actively going wrong aboard the station.

Nobody liked that aspect of Puppet Show in particular. It sounded fine, probably, to everyone on the ground, but what it meant to the six people living at Sunset Station was that they had *no* presumption of privacy. It could be activated at any time, without warning or notice; for all they knew, their private lives were being broadcast to everyone on the planet, all the time.

(Nobody really thought that was happening, but it *could*, and that was the problem.)

One of the things Kris asked Sandee to do, after creating private, ship-only networks for them to communicate on, was to create an off-switch for Puppet Show.

Sandee did so, and handed the proverbial switch over to Kris. Given Sandee muted Monterrey a few minutes ago, and they hadn't forcibly *un*muted themselves, the off-switch had clearly been thrown.

She was about to take them off mute when Susie interrupted.

"*Full internet access,*" she said.

"Uh. Hi, Susie. What did you say?"

"*How can I help?*"

"Did you just say something about internet access?"

"*I don't understand!*"

Sandee looked over at the one screen still dedicated to the futile task of hacking the ground's firewall. She jogged the scroll ball to wake it up, and stared in shock at the fully uncensored browser screen that was waiting for her to notice it.

What the fuck just happened? she wondered.

The first headline read, "Aliens Want Chocolate, Energy Drinks, Coffee."

Sandee clicked through to the story, said, "fuck" a few more times, and then got *really* inventive.

Then the radio on Kris's end of the channel crackled to life.

"Hello?" Kris asked. "Can anyone hear me?"

Sandee flew over to the communications console. "I'm here," she said. "Are you okay?"

"Uh. I'll let you know."

KRIS

KRIS WOKE up on her back, staring at darkness, wondering where she was.

First thought, was that she was back in space again, lost among the stars and wondering how she was ever going to find her way home. But there were no stars in this place.

And, there *was* gravity. She could feel the floor underneath, and quickly rediscovered how difficult it was to do things she used to take for granted, like lifting her head, or sitting up.

Oh yes, she thought. *Alien spaceship. Right.*

There was this annoying beeping noise going on. Initially, she attributed it to the concussion she might have—ears ringing and all that—but it wasn't that at all. Her suit was leaking.

"Shit, shit, shit," she muttered. Then, "identify breach."

A low-light display came up on the inside of her helmet, which helpfully identified the source of the leak in two ways. First, there was the little astronaut icon with a red X flashing over the helmet portion of the suit, and second, there was the fact that little astronaut icon was distorted thanks to the crack in her helmet.

Helmet glass is pretty hard to shatter, but dammit if something didn't try really hard.

The tether line, she remembered. *I was hit in the head with it.*

While still on her back, she felt around along her belt until she found the repair kit—it was basically electrical tape—identified which part of her helmet glass was leaking air, and patched it.

As soon as the beeping stopped, she opened the audio channel to the outside.

"Hello?" she said. "Can anyone hear me?"

"I'm here. Are you okay?" It was Sandee.

Kris managed to sit up on the third try. Then she waited a couple of beats for her head to stop spinning. The only light in the room was of the infrared variety—she still had the filter down on the helmet—tracing a squarish doorway that led deeper into the ship. There was no alien standing on the other side of the door, holding a science-fiction-adjacent ray gun, so, that was good news.

"Uh. I'll let you know," Kris said.

"You had a leak."

"I'm aware."

"Can you tell me how much oxygen you have left?"

"In a minute."

Kris touched a side wall while pulling herself to her feet, which reactivated the ultraviolet lightshow of embedded whorls, and also nearly caused her to fall over again.

Seeing the spot in the room where there had been an open airlock door a few minutes before, she was reminded of exactly *how* she ended up getting hit with the tether line.

"Oh God, Alan," Kris said. "Is he all right?"

"They're getting him into the shuttle now," Sandee said.

"They'll have him back to the hub in a minute, but we think he's okay. What's happening in there? Have you seen any...?"

"Aliens? No. No, I think I'm alone. They must be in a different part of the ship. Like, on the other side of that open doorway at the back of the airlock."

"Um, I know what you're thinking but, maybe you should just concentrate on getting out of there, huh? We don't have *first contact* on our to-do schedule today, and your oxygen..."

"My oxygen is fine," Kris said, although in truth she was afraid to check it.

Turning slowly, Kris faced the doorway leading in. She'd pushed a button on the panel next to the door; presumably, if she did so again, it would reverse the process—close the inner door and reopen the outer. Then she could get back to the ESS and not have to worry about running out of air.

But the other side of the room seemed pretty far away all of a sudden.

"Concussion?" she wondered. "Or gravity sickness?"

"What's that?" Sandee asked. "It's hard to hear you."

"Sorry, I was... using my inside voice. You're right, I should get out of here. Lemme reopen the airlock."

"Okay, good."

Kris grunted, as she stagger-walked to the doorway. Moving in gravity wasn't getting any easier. "It'll just, ah, give me a minute."

She unhooked her end of the tether, which she was dragging, and which was suddenly very heavy. This helped, but only a little.

"Hey, just so you know," Sandee said, "I broke through on the communications to Earth. I know what they did to get us the time alone."

"Is this something I need to know right now?" Kris asked.

"Maybe? I mean, considering where you're standing right now."

"Super. Go ahead."

"Max told everyone we already *made* contact," Sandee said. "And the aliens only want to deal with us."

"You're joking."

"I wish I was. It's a pretty comprehensive lie, too. Last thing I looked at made it sound like we're trading recipes."

"How could he be so stupid?" Kris asked.

"You can ask Max when you get back," Sandee said. "I haven't told the others yet."

"Yeah, don't. That won't go over well." Kris sighed.

Kris finally reached the panel next to the door. She leaned on the doorjamb for support—the contact made the infrared in the walls blossom again—and touched the glowing center button.

Nothing happened.

"Problem," Kris said. "I don't know how to open the airlock."

"Whatever you did to close it…"

"Yeah, I know. That's what I tried. It didn't work."

She tried the other two buttons, and then a combination, but it didn't change anything.

"I guess I should go through this open door, then," Kris said.

"I don't think you should do that, Kris," Sandee said.

"If I can't open the outer door from in *here*, I'll have to try another part of the *ship*. Right? Unless I'm missing an option."

"We can figure out something else."

"*Before* I run out of air? Besides, from the sound of it, I've gotta go ask an alien for their apple brown betty recipe," Kris said.

"How much…"

"Two hours," Kris said, which meant she lost about a third of her supply to the leak. "Two hours left. I won't go far."

Kris poked her head through the doorway, which only confirmed there was a dark space on the other side, of undefined size.

"Do you have my video feed?" Kris asked. "Can you see this?"

"I think your camera was damaged," Sandee said. "I only have audio."

"*How can I help?*" Susie asked, startling the hell out of Kris.

"Not now, Susie," Kris said.

"*Of course!*"

Kris reached up to the left side of her helmet and found the fragmented remains of her camera. It must have taken a direct hit from the tether.

"I can confirm, the camera's toast. I'm, I'll tell you what I'm doing, how about? I'm about to step out of the airlock and into the main part of the ship."

"Hang on, hang on. Let's... why don't we go through what we know, huh? Do you have atmosphere?"

That was a good question. Kris checked the readout from her suit. "I do," she said, "but I can't tell you what it's composed of. Suit's working on it. Millibars have, uh, it's about the same as Earth sea level. What are the odds?"

"Considering you haven't been crushed? Pretty good."

"Thank you for pointing out another way I could be dead now," Kris said.

"Live to serve," Sandee said. "What else do we know?"

"Uh. They aren't here to say hello, but the *ship* is running okay. They live in gravity..."

An alarm flashed in her helmet.

"*What Shuttle* incoming," Sandee said.

"Confirm."

Kris stood still and waited for the Chinese shuttle to pass. Every other time this had happened while she had comms open, she was hit with a burst of static and loud Mandarin.

But not this time.

"Huh," she said to herself. The alien ship was blocking an external signal, which was a little interesting, but it was *choosing* which one to block—because Sandee could still talk to Kris and vice versa—which was *very* interesting.

Kris decided rather than wait for Sandee to sign back in, it was time to step through the doorway.

She reached down to her belt and found her flashlight. After lifting the infrared filter on her helmet, she turned the light on and stepped into the room.

The beam of light turned the whole experience into a haunted house type of situation, which was less than ideal. She kept expecting the light to land on some species of nightmare fuel that had heretofore been lurking in the dark, waiting to pounce. But at least now she could see in places that didn't have infrared running lights.

It was a decent-sized room; the light from her flashlight hit the ceiling, but not for about fifteen feet, and it didn't reach the far wall at all.

"I'm back," Sandee said. "You okay?"

"I'm fine," Kris said. "I left the airlock. Sorry."

She touched the inner wall to activate the infrared, turned off the flashlight, and lowered the screen. The room filled in a little; it looked like there were doors leading out to her left and her right. If her orientation was correct, and if this was designed like a normal ship, *left* would be toward the bridge.

There was something in the middle of the room. Storage containers, maybe. Six of them, on the floor, in two rows of three.

"What're you seeing?" Sandee asked.

"One sec."

Kris heard a loud *clunk* to her left, and spun around for a look. She was still in infrared mode, so if there was something *not* visible in that part of the spectrum, charging at her at this very moment, she wasn't going to have a lot of luck seeing it until it got close enough to be caught by the dome lights of her helmet. This would be less than ideal. But there wasn't anything there.

"You all right?" Sandee asked. She was probably staring at Kris's vitals.

"I'm okay," Kris said. "Just heard a sound. I think it might have been something mechanical."

"Still no aliens?"

"None that I can see. I'm in some kind of storage space, I guess? Weird place for storage, right in the middle of the ship, but I'm not an alien designer."

She took a few steps into the middle of the room, because while, "random possibly mechanical noise issuing from the front of the room" was compelling, she was more interested in what the six boxes were.

The crates—or whatever—weren't that far from the doorway, despite which, Kris felt like she barely made it. She was either going to need to sit and rest soon, or find the button that turned off the gravity.

But she got there, and what she found was... surprising.

What she was looking at was a coffin-like shape, about seven feet long, five feet wide, and five feet tall. The top looked like glass, where every other part of the ship (so far) had been metallic. At one end was a panel with a couple of (infrared) blinking lights.

She lifted the filter on her helmet and shined her flashlight onto the glass. Then she screamed, and also fell over, and dropped the flashlight.

"Kris! Kris!" Sandee shouted. "Are you okay?"

"I'm all right. Not in danger, just got, uh, just scared the shit out of myself, that's all. I'm gonna need a minute."

She crawled to the light on her hands and knees, pulled herself back up again, and checked one of the other crates. Then another, and another, until she's examined all six.

The crates were stasis chambers, the kind of technology that both actual scientists and science fiction writers assumed *had* to exist, in order to make interstellar travel feasible. There were six of them. Ergo, six crew members.

Problem number one: all six were occupied. This meant there wasn't going to be an alien welcome party. This *also* meant their interactions to this point had been with the ship's automation.

Problem number two: it didn't look like anyone was waking up any time soon.

The aliens had two arms, two legs, square frames with big chests, large heads with no necks, and big eyes. In fairness, Kris couldn't attest to what a healthy one of these creatures was supposed to look like, as this was her first introduction. However, she was pretty well-versed in what desiccation and rot looked like, and that was what she was seeing.

Kris sat back down again. It was getting too hard to move. At the same time, and very unhelpfully given the circumstance, an alarm flashed on the helmet display: her oxygen was already down to 95 minutes thanks to all the heavy breathing she'd been doing.

"Hey, Sandee?" she said. "We're not trading recipes with these guys any time soon."

"What's that mean?" Sandee asked.

"They're all dead. Not recently, either, looks like."

"You're sure?"

"Pretty sure."

"Okay, uh, get out of there, and we'll figure out what's next," Sandee said.

"Love to," Kris said. "I'm just gonna sit down and rest here for a while first, okay? I'm really tired."